UNWAVERING HOPE

THE HOPE SERIES
BOOK 3

NELIANNE GENNER

fhp
FIREFLY HILL PRESS

BOOKS IN THE HOPE SERIES

To everyone out there who strives for acceptance.
Hold onto hope.

1

ASHTON

James Taylor once said, "You have to choose whether to love yourself or not." If I learned nothing else in the last five years, I learned this. Insecurity and self-doubt consumed me to the point where I almost lost myself completely. And it wasn't until I felt the ground beneath me crumbling that I finally had an epiphany. I knew there were two roads I could take. One would lead me further into darkness, and the other would lead me to the potential of profound happiness. When I finally reached the proverbial fork, it was the clarity I gained from my experiences that showed me the way, like the sun breaking through a storm-battered sky.

Developing feelings for my best friend Riley brought out a piece of me I didn't know existed, but developing feelings for *Kira*, who Louis had pretended to be, brought me to a place of comfort. And when I found out I had been lied to, and that the reason for the deception was based on fear, I realized that nobody was going to accept me until I accepted myself. Another person would never feel safe with me until I felt comfortable in my own skin. It was difficult to learn, but I knew the lesson would repeat itself until it ultimately sunk in.

IN SPITE of our ups and downs, Louis and I continued to work together at the Tap House. He was there every weekend without fail, and after a few months, he and I were able to salvage a sense of former friendship. I knew we'd never be super close, that I'd never trust him the way I did when I was talking with him as *Kira* through Instagram, but I also knew what he did wasn't malicious. Deep down, Louis was a good person. He just wasn't *my* person.

However, I would be eternally grateful for the relationship I had with *Kira*. Even though she wasn't real, the conversations I had with her were. I had never been able to open up to someone like that before, and I'd always hold a special place in my heart for the short time I spent getting to know her and letting her get to know me in return. I would also be grateful for the recommendation of the sun lamp, which proved to be very effective in helping with my seasonal depression. Louis was pleased to know he'd helped me in some way by suggesting I use one during the winter months.

As far as online friends were concerned, I pretty much stopped chatting with people I didn't know on social media. And it wasn't just because I'd been catfished. I wanted to find a connection with someone through the vibes I felt in person, rather than through a screen. Since I didn't have buddies I could go out with like a lot of guys my age did, it was difficult to meet new people at places one might expect. But I decided I had to come out of my shell a little and engage in conversation whenever an opportunity presented itself. Sometimes, that was during a shift at the Tap House, like how I met Louis. Sometimes, it was while I was working out at Planet Fitness. And sometimes, it was when I was at my new full-time job at the hospital.

That's right! I scored myself a position at Doylestown Hospital working as a respiratory therapist. They were so impressed with me during my rotations that they asked me to become a permanent part of the team. This made me happy for several reasons, one of them being that the team included Kendal, who had become like another sister to me. Another reason was the hospital was so close to where Sophia and Owen lived, so I could just drop by and see them even more often than I had before. And the last reason I was so happy was that I was doing something I truly loved and was good at, which gave me a lot of confidence, a true blessing when confidence was something I'd lacked for so long. It wasn't always easy being the baby of the family, suffering from depression, and constantly worrying about the judgment and acceptance of others. It was brutal out there. But I finally felt like I had found my bearings.

I'd only been at the hospital for a month, but I was able to see myself there for years to come. I worked mostly in pediatrics, which I preferred, especially when being an uncle to Liam and Hope had really made me grow a love for being around small children. And I always had the opportunity to meet new people, whether it was a patient or a coworker, and that was one part of the job I thoroughly enjoyed.

Due to gaining full-time employment, I could only squeeze in one shift a week at the Tap House since I was on the schedule a few times a week at the hospital. I could have quit altogether, but my attachment to the staff and the atmosphere at the restaurant was strong. Other than that, I spent my time at the gym and with family, as per usual.

I briefly dated a girl this past spring who I'd met at the Tap House. She expressed interest when she came in for dinner with her girlfriends, flirting a little throughout the meal while I was serving them and then slipped me her number before they left. I liked her assertiveness, so I waited a day and gave her a call. We went on a few dates, and she turned out to be very cool and interesting, but I didn't feel the two of us had the chemistry I was looking for in a relationship. She agreed with my take on things, so there were no hard feelings.

Since then, I had just been keeping myself open and remaining comfortable with who I was as a person and what I wanted in this world. I would find my person when I was supposed to. My brother, Oliver, had to move to the other side of the country to find his better half, but I was hoping mine would be a bit more local.

After all, I had double the chances of meeting my soulmate on any given day, right?

2

SOPHIA

It was the end of June, and my wedding to Owen was only three months away. Only one year ago, we got engaged in Bonaire, and I couldn't believe how fast the time was soaring by. And there was still so much to get through before the big day. Sometime between July and August would be my bridal shower, and thanks to Paityn and my mom, I was kept completely in the dark, aside from the fact I'd voiced my preference of a beach theme. Additionally, I had two more dress fittings, we had to finalize our music selections, Owen and I had to meet with the priest one last time, and we both still had to figure out what we were doing for our bachelor and bachelorette parties.

Hot pink limo, anyone?

The thirtieth of September would be here in a blink of an eye. I had to keep reminding myself to calm down, pace myself, and just enjoy the ride. I wished I was more like Paityn was when she had gotten engaged. She planned her wedding to Bradley in under a year and stayed pretty chill about the whole thing. Her laid-back personality definitely made me envious over the years, and I really wanted to borrow it for these next few months. Instead, my anxiety was getting the best of me, and I repeatedly thought about all the things that could possibly go wrong, so much so that it was keeping me up at night.

What if the flowers don't look the way I imagined them? What if it rains on the day of the wedding? What if I end up putting on a few pounds and look awful in my dress? What if I hate my hair and makeup? What if Owen gets cold feet and changes his mind?

My mom told me these were all valid concerns of any bride in the months leading up to the big day, but that didn't ease my mind. I still felt like any and all of it could happen. But I was taking it day by day and really trying to hope for the best.

Aside from worrying about the wedding planning, things were going well. The photography business was booming, Bowie had grown into a beautiful dog, who was about to celebrate her second birthday in August, and all was currently calm on the family front. Oliver and Chloe would be flying in for the wedding, which was great because we hadn't seen them since last Christmas. Elijah, Bethany, and Hope were around frequently. It was hard to believe Hope was going to turn four years old right before we got married.

Where does the time go?

Of course, we asked her to be our flower girl, and she very graciously and excitedly accepted. We asked Liam to be the ring bearer, and he was more than ready to take on the task. Liam loved receiving special jobs, whether it was at school or at home, so this was right up his alley.

A little over six months ago, Paityn and Bradley had

Liam evaluated by a specialist to see if there was more of a diagnosis than the receptive expressive language disorder. When they concluded the testing, Liam's doctor reported that he did in fact have ASD (autism spectrum disorder). My sister took the news extremely well, since she had already been told by the pediatrician this might be the case, and Liam had been exhibiting certain behaviors over the years that prepared her, such as his attachment to her, the occasional flapping of his hands when he got excited, agitation whenever there was a break in his routines, and his distaste for loud sounds. It didn't hurt that we had a special education teacher as a mom and that Liam already had an IEP (Individualized Education Plan) with specially designed instruction and related services. His case manager at school updated his learning goals with this additional diagnosis to set him up for success.

Paityn and Bradley were doing a great job meeting his needs at home too. Brad stopped spending so much time at the restaurant in order to be with Liam more and support my sister. With some new hires and a greater number of delegated responsibilities, the restaurant was bustling. And best of all, Liam still had Doug!

We can't forget about Doug. That bunny is a star in that house and makes an appearance on every family Zoom call. As he should.

We got to see Doug every time they came to town. No way would they leave home without him. And the next time would be for the wedding week. After that, they'd be back for Christmastime, as usual, and then Easter too. It'd become a tradition for Bradley's family to visit them at Thanksgiving, which worked well, since I had been doing that holiday with Owen's family.

My soon-to-be in-laws! Ahhh! I can't believe Raelyn is actually going to be my sister. I'm still having trouble wrapping my head around that particular new adaptation, but it's so exciting!

"THE EVENT COORDINATOR from Parx is going to be here any minute!" Owen shouted softly from outside the bathroom door.

"I know, I know... I'm almost ready. I just have to finish getting dressed. Can you run Bowie out front to go potty?" I could hear her whimpering and knew she needed to go.

"Got it! Just make it quick. I don't want to keep her waiting in the studio," Owen said.

I slipped my black high rise capri slacks on over a white bodysuit and added a cute mint green blazer. I threw on a pair of sandals as I fluffed my hair in the mirror, slicked on some lip gloss, and hurried off to the studio. Luckily, Owen was already sitting at his desk, ready and waiting. The doorbell rang just minutes later, and I opened the door to greet the coordinator, Bowie wagging her tail by my feet.

"Claire, hello, come on in," I said to her as I ushered her in. "Welcome to our photography studio. It's small, but it's all ours."

"Thank you, Sophia. So nice to be here. How are you?" she asked.

"We're well," Owen said, walking out from behind his desk to shake her hand. "How are you? It's great to have you here."

"I'm doing just fine. The place is lovely. And you do all of your consultations here?" she asked us, looking around at what we had to offer.

"Most of the time, yes, unless we have a client far away and they prefer to do a video call or meet at a halfway point," I explained.

"Very nice. Well, let's get down to business. Shall we?" Claire slowly stepped over to our studio table and grabbed a seat. Pulling a tasteful folder embossed with the Parx's logo from her brown leather briefcase and opening it up, she signaled for us to join her.

Owen and I sat down, eager to hear her pitch. We knew there was another job she wanted to hire us for, but we had no idea what it was or when it was. Our assumptions were that it would be a big name and it'd be happening over the next few months. As long as it wasn't happening on the wedding weekend or the week we were going away for the honeymoon, we were in! That was, of course, if nothing else was booked either. We had become experts at avoiding double-bookings after the fiasco we had with having to split up for those two events when Owen forgot to look at our calendar before accepting a job.

"I have a concert I would love for the two of you to work, but it's in October. Is that too short of notice?" She searched our faces with concern in her eyes.

"We do have a few things booked in the second half of October, but let's check the calendar and compare dates." I picked up Owen's iPad and tapped on the apps until I pulled up our electronic schedule. I knew there was a chance we'd have to decline because of how popular our growing business had become, but I was hopeful we'd be able to squeeze this in.

Claire shared the date with us and the artist, and lucky for us, we had only one event that weekend, and it was on a Sunday.

We are free! Thank God!

"We accept!" I exclaimed, unable to hide my enthusiasm. "Count us in!"

I'm going to meet Kelsea Ballerini! Is this my life now? If so, I'll take it.

3

ASHTON

"Come over here, please?" I stared into my sweet angel's beautiful brown eyes. "Listen to me." She stared back, letting me know I had her full attention. "You need to learn how to play nice. You can't keep taking every toy. We share in this family." I pretended she understood every word I was saying, as well as any puppy can comprehend what their owners are telling them.

She sat down on the carpet beside my legs. I knew she felt bad, but I had to stand firm in my discipline. "If you can't share, you can't play at all. Understood?" She nuzzled into me, begging for forgiveness. "I'm going to give one to Bowie, and then I'll give another to you. Leave her be."

Mabel took her toy and kept a distance of about four to five feet from Bowie as she played. I sat down and dove back into my book, keeping an eye on the two of them with every turn of the page. I was really into reading romance novels these days. They helped me figure out the type of relationship I really wanted to have with someone.

"Hey!" I shouted when Bowie and Mabel began

wrestling. "Take it easy." Mabel ran over and jumped up on the couch next to me, seeking approval. I placed the book down on the coffee table, temporarily, and brought her in for some warm snuggles, and I couldn't help but smile with gratitude.

Mom and Dad finally gave in and got another dog. It took a while after the loss of Harley, but eventually they decided the house was too empty without a four-legged friend. Even with Bowie's frequent visits and overnight stays, it just wasn't the same. They got her in the spring, and it took a few days to name her, but after spending time with the pup and realizing how affectionate she was, they went with the name, Mabel, which actually meant "lovable."

Mabel was a yellow Labrador Retriever, just like Harley was, and she was just as great of a dog. They had minor differences in their personalities, but they were both loyal and easy to train. The addition was not only right for my parents, but it was helpful to me as well. Having her around was a mood booster and made me feel comfortable and safe. Dogs gave you unconditional love you just didn't get from anywhere else. And when I needed her, she was there. Mabel could always tell when I was down or stressed and would be at my side in an instant. When she and Bowie were together, I had a double dose of emotional support.

What more could I ask for?

I HAD to work that night at the hospital, a twelve-hour shift that began at seven. I slid into my light blue scrubs, brushed my teeth, fixed my hair, and said goodbye to the girls and my mom, who were all sitting outside enjoying the cool evening breeze. We had Bowie until the next day because Sophia and Owen had a photography gig that was going late into the night. Dad hadn't arrived home yet from work, but since my mom was home, I didn't have to put anyone in a crate. I always hated that part. The sad puppy dog eyes were just too much to take.

The drive to work was always smooth and thankfully brief. I never let myself forget how fortunate I was to have such a good job so close to home. Hopefully, I'd be there until I retired. That was the dream. And then in forty years, my spouse and I would travel around the world together. Assuming I ended up married. And assuming they liked to travel.

Wow. Don't get ahead of yourself.

I clocked in, shoved my belongings in my locker, and headed out to check my assignment. While I was looking at the board for my name, I felt the presence of someone lurking behind me. I turned quickly to catch Kendal with a hand out, ready to grab me at my right side.

"You're working tonight too?" I asked, instinctually backing away and swatting at her pinching fingers.

"Yeah, seven to seven. I take it you have the same shift?" she responded.

"Yup! It looks like we'll be here all night together again. Fun!" I laughed.

"Let me check my assignment. I'm praying I get to work with this one male nurse I have my eye on," Kendal exclaimed.

"A male nurse? What's his name?" I looked again at the board, trying not to sound too curious.

I'm always up for some eye candy.

"I don't know his name yet. He's new. I think he's a

nurse, but he could be in another department." She shrugged her shoulders. "Oh well, duty calls!"

"Great story!" I called out facetiously as she trotted away.

I hardly ever worked side by side with Kendal, but on occasion, we were assigned to the same floor. Usually, it was in the pediatrics unit, which I loved above all others. Tonight, I was assigned there, but she wasn't. I hoped to get the scoop from her later on whether or not she made contact with the hottie.

When I got to pediatrics, there were already a few employees looking at charts and discussing the stats and medical interventions of the babies. I approached them to collect a clipboard and listened in on responsibilities that had to be taken. One asked me to help with monitoring and recording progress of the patients in the infant room, and after that, I switched gears to consult with a physician about some of the respiratory conditions we were seeing and their respective treatment plans.

Around midnight, I really needed a pick-me-up, especially when I had seven more hours to go on my shift, so I went to the cafeteria to buy a very necessary cup of coffee. While I was there, Kendal walked in to grab a bottle of water.

"Fancy seeing you here!" she said as she sidled up next to me in line.

"I need some caffeine. How have the last few hours been for you?"

"Pretty decent, actually! I caught a glimpse of the dreamboat I mentioned earlier. I still haven't talked to him, but the night is young, am I right?"

I chuckled and shuffled ahead in the queue. "Well, good

luck with that! You better give me all the tea if anything happens." I told her, taking a sip from my cup.

"And here I thought you only drank coffee," she said with a smirk.

"I'll catch you later. Break time is over!" I left her and hopped on the nearest elevator.

Maybe I'll find someone here that catches my eye too.

I spent the next few hours running diagnostic tests and completing necessary paperwork and charting. The job was far from glamorous, but I wouldn't trade it. This place was where I was meant to be. I could feel it in my bones. And, for the most part, I was happy.

SEVEN O'CLOCK in the morning came, and the sun was shining brightly as I walked to my car, shades on, in dire need of some rest. The yawns were coming approximately every thirty seconds at this point. I ate an energy bar to help me from falling asleep on the drive back to the house, as I did after every twelve-hour shift. Thoughts of jumping into bed with not one, but two yellow furballs, flooded my mind. I parked in the driveway and ran inside, saying hello to my dad, who was in the kitchen packing up his lunch for work that day.

We were like two ships passing in the night.

Both Mabel and Bowie sensed my return and were at my side within minutes. With a whistle and quick wave, I gestured for them to follow me to my bedroom, and they complied without hesitation. Within minutes, the three of us were peacefully wrapped together, drifting off to dreamland.

And what a spectacular place my dreams can be! There,

I can be with anyone, never worrying about coming up with strategies to find out if someone likes me or if they like men or if they have a problem with me being bisexual. In my dreams, I have what I want, usually. There are times when my dreams turn to nightmares. But I think that's just my real life fears making their way into my subconscious.

4

SOPHIA

The wedding was now less than three months away. And we still had Owen and Bowie's birthdays to celebrate over the summer too. How in the world was I going to get everything done? I had tried to handle most of it myself, getting input here and there, like on the day I found my dress and the bridesmaids' dresses with Rae and Kendal and on the day I selected my flowers, which Paityn helped me decide on via FaceTime. Owen was working with me on the music. But I needed some additional support. I was going to have to leave the bachelorette party planning up to the girls, and Mom would have to help me with wedding favors, centerpieces, and place cards for the reception, as well as attending my next dress fitting with me.

That's what moms are for, right?

A text message was sent to let her know what I still needed to get done, and I asked her kindly for her assistance with all of it. I knew she would want to be there for me, but I never wanted to assume I could just drop things in her lap, or anyone's for that matter. I patiently waited for a text back with confirmation while I played fetch with Bowie in the living room.

We really need a bigger place.

Running around with a ball, my phone alerted me I had a message. I took my cell out of my back pocket and went to respond. And it was at that moment, I felt a twinge on my left side. I sat down on the couch nearby, holding my side in pain. Bowie jumped up, sinking into the cushions with me, and she offered her best snuggles, in an effort to comfort me.

"I'm sure I'll be alright, girl. It's probably just something I ate."

She curled up next to me with her head on my lap, clearly skeptical. I didn't fully believe I was okay either, but I was trying to remain hopeful. The twinge came again, this time sharper.

Maybe it's my ovaries? Could I have a cyst? Am I ovulating? What the heck is going on?

I read the text on my phone, which was in fact from my mom, telling me she was willing to assist me with whatever I needed. I thanked her and then informed her of this sudden pain and asked for her opinion. She had some guesses, similar to what I thought, along with asking if I did any strenuous exercises recently, but she suggested I call my doctor if it didn't subside in the next hour.

I don't think playing with a dog counts as doing any kind of strenuous exercise.

I sat on the couch for a while with Bowie, praying the pain would go away. When over an hour passed and it was still just as present, I called my doctor. Immediately, they suggested I go over to the emergency room and be checked out. Owen was over at the Taylor residence helping his dad get things ready to take down to their boat for an upcoming fishing trip, but luckily, the pain wasn't so bad that I couldn't drive the three minutes it took to get to the hospital. I let my mom know the plan, bid farewell to my fluffy girl, and sped off in the direction of the emergency room.

I found a spot close to the entrance and slowly walked to the doors of the expansive hospital while on the phone with Owen. He was going to meet me there momentarily. I was mildly concerned that something serious was happening, but I continued to try and convince myself it had to be something I ate. Within minutes of checking in at the front desk, a nurse was calling me back to gather information and assess the situation.

"Sophia, you are having some pain on your left side? How long has it been going on?" The nurse asked me while she quickly typed into the computer screen.

"Yes, right here." I showed her by rubbing the area without pressing on it. "And I would say it has been going on for a little less than two hours."

"Is the pain sporadic, or is it steady?" she asked me, continuing to tap away on the keyboard, typing what I just shared.

"It was sporadic at first, but it has been steady for maybe the last thirty minutes. Do you think it's something serious?" I began to panic.

"We won't know anything until the doctor sees you and runs some tests. But don't worry until you have to." That's what Dad always said, that I shouldn't worry until there was a reason to worry. He used that method as a way to calm my anxiety and prevent attacks. It usually helped, but sometimes I got in my head.

After the nurse asked me a few additional questions, she brought me back to a room with a bed, where I was asked to change into a gown that tied in the back and told they'd need a urine sample. I filled the cup and gave it to the nurse. A doctor appeared soon after.

"We are going to do an ultrasound as soon as they have an opening. In the meantime, lay here and try to relax. Try to drink some of the water the nurses brought to you. You need to have a full stomach." The doctor left and closed the curtain to the room behind him. I attempted to make myself comfortable under the blankets, which were pretty warm.

All I could think about was what could possibly be wrong with me. My dad had issues with his colon for years and later found out it was diverticulitis, and Elijah was diagnosed with celiac disease, so my mind began to run wild with ideas of there being a problem with my colon too. On the other hand, I wondered if it was my kidneys or my ovaries. I gave myself several reminders not to pick up my phone and do a search on Google for severe pain on your left side, knowing that would just make my anxiety worse.

Let the doctors do their thing, Sophia. Relax.

Just as I almost dozed off, Owen showed up at the door. "How's my favorite patient doing?" He pulled the chair over from against the wall closer to my bed.

"Okay, I guess. Much better now that you're here!"

"Where are they at with things? Does the doctor know what's causing the pain yet?"

"No, not yet. A nurse took a urine sample, so that's being tested now, and then I'm going to have an ultrasound done. That should help identify the culprit."

Ouch. There it is again.

I reached out for Owen's hand and squeezed it tighter than I ever had. "Do you think it's something serious? I'm scared."

"Understandable. I doubt I'd be too calm in the same

situation, but let's just see what happens. It could be something minor that's easily treated."

I took several deep breaths in and out, still holding Owen's hand.

He's right. It's possible this is nothing.

"Yeah, maybe I drank something that is causing some gastrointestinal problems, and I'll be fine in a few days. I hope so anyway."

After another half an hour, the nurse returned to take me for the ultrasound. Owen offered to hold my hand the whole way, but I told him to hang out and watch television. No need for both of us to be traipsing around the hospital, exposed to even more germs. After being hustled through two long hallways, my gurney was turned into a small dark room where apparently the magic happened.

The technician conducted her imaging of my stomach, and I lay there dying of ridiculous pain and curiosity.

"Do you see anything alarming? Anything you can share with me? Am I alright?" I asked her with panic in my voice and worry filling me from every strand of hair in my head to the nail polish on my toes.

"Well, the doctor will hopefully be able to give you a more definitive diagnosis after he looks over everything, but I can tell you that, from what I'm seeing, your ovaries look normal, and your kidneys look fine. Try not to worry yourself sick."

Easy for her to say.

"That's good to hear, I guess. But I know something is wrong somewhere. I wouldn't be in this much pain over nothing." I looked up to the ceiling as my eyes filled up with fear.

"Try to calm down, honey. We have very good doctors here. I'm confident you'll get the answers you're looking for." And with that, she handed me a tissue and proceeded to wheel me back down to the emergency room, where I found Owen waiting with a smile. Looking at his face made me feel like everything was going to turn out okay, no matter what.

WE WATCHED two episodes of *Friends* before we saw the doctor, but when he walked in the room, a wave of relief crashed over me. I didn't even know what the results were, but knowing I was about to find out the problem eased my nerves.

"I looked at the images from your ultrasound." He prepared me for the news. "The good news here is that everything looks healthy with your kidneys and your ovaries, which rules some things out for us." He sat down in a chair across from me, looking over my paperwork.

"And the bad news then?" Beads of sweat prickled on the back of my neck and moistened my palms. Owen leaned over from the left of me and put his right hand on my thigh.

"Breathe, Sophia. Breathe," he said soothingly.

"I don't have any conclusive data yet that could provide an exact diagnosis, but it would appear your colon is highly inflamed. I'm going to recommend you see a gastroenterologist over the next few months, and I'm sending you home with a list of foods you need to stay away from, at least until that appointment."

"What does all of this mean? Am I sick? Will I need surgery at some point?" Tears spilled over my lashes and fell down to my chin.

This can't be happening right now.

"We have nothing conclusive that indicates you are sick.

This could be anything from a meal that inflamed your colon to colitis or possibly something a bit more serious, but try not to let your fears run away with you. And try to stay off of WebMD. That website will have you believing you've already got one foot in the grave," the doctor said with a light chuckle as the last word left his mouth.

He handed me the paperwork with the referral for the gastroenterologist, a list of foods I needed to avoid, and a prescription to help relieve the inflammation. I thanked him and promised to make the appointment right way, especially since they booked at least three months out. Once he was gone, I took another deep breath in and out and looked to Owen for reassurance.

"Try to relax. You'll make the appointment, you'll follow the dietary restrictions, and you'll take the medicine he prescribed. Everything is going to be okay. And if something does turn out to be more serious, we'll cross that bridge when we come to it." Owen leaned in and kissed me on my forehead.

"You're right. I shouldn't worry until or if I have to, just like my dad always says." Daniel's voice echoed in my head. "And as long as I know I have you, I can get through anything." I smiled at Owen, expressing an unwavering hope in his ability to always make me safe and protected.

He lined his right wrist up next to my left wrist. "You see these tattoos?" I brought my stare to our crescent moons we each had permanently inked on our bodies. "When we went and got them after we got back from Bonaire, we promised to always be there for each other, no matter what."

"I remember," I told him. "We're connected for life." A single tear fell from my eyes just seconds later.

"Now, let's get you dressed. We have some wedding duties to get back to!" He helped me out of bed. "I was thinking that after we stop at the pharmacy, we could go take your ring to get resized and find a band for me, if you're up for it."

"Yes! But only if we can stop home to get changed and then take out a canoe on the lake afterwards. Please?" I stood there in my hospital gown with a pouty face.

"Of course, we can. It's a beautiful day, and you know I'd do anything to cheer you up," he said, wrapping his arms around me.

"Great! Let's get out of here!"

I was going to miss my engagement ring for a couple of weeks, but I had lost some weight trying to shed for the big day, so it really didn't fit. I couldn't have it falling off. And we really needed to get Owen a nice band that he would never want to take off.

"I'M SO glad you're feeling better now," Owen said as we were pulling the canoe into the water. "Those anti-inflammatory pills worked fast!"

"They really did!" I told him, trying to finagle myself into the seat. "And I'm also feeling a little better about the wedding, now that you finally have a ring picked out."

"I knew it would be easy for me. I wanted something simple but classy," he responded, joining me in the small boat.

"Getting you a tungsten band was the right call. Now I won't have to worry about you scratching it up with all your physical activity," I said, smiling over at him.

"I'll take good care of it, Soph, just like you have with your engagement ring." He stretched his legs out in front of him.

"I'm already missing it!" I looked down at my left hand. "My finger feels so naked."

"It won't take too long for the jeweler to resize and polish it," he reassured me. "They said it would be two weeks at the most!"

"I know, and then on the big day, I'll get to have its matching wedding band to go with it!"

"Nothing but the best for my girl!" He tilted his head back and gave me one of those gorgeous grins he has mastered over the years. And at that moment, I forgot all about being in the hospital.

Sophia was in the hospital yesterday, so I wanted to stop by and check on her. I made a quick coffee run and drove over to visit her and Owen in the studio. When I pulled open the front door, I was greeted by Bowie, which was always a nice bonus, and she led me back to where Owen and Sophia were adding photos to their themed album books they displayed for clients.

"How's the patient today? Feeling any better?" I asked Sophia, handing her a coffee and then sliding one over to Owen on the desk where they sat working.

"I'm doing okay. The pain in my left side seems to have subsided for the most part. I started taking the medicine immediately, and I was surprised with how quickly it brought relief.

"And that's for inflammation, right? Be careful of what you eat," I told her, realizing afterward that she probably had already been given those very detailed instructions.

"Yes, thank you, Mr. Medical Professional. Will do!" she joked.

"You can catch up with Ashton for a bit if you want. I

can handle this," Owen offered while sliding prints into the clear pages of the Sweet Escape book.

"Thanks! I have to give Bowie some water anyway." Sophia stood up and began walking toward the apartment. "Come on, girl. Uncle Ashton wants to play fetch." She turned back to look at me with a playful smirk. Sophia, that is, not Bowie. Although, I'm sure Bowie was thinking about how I just got bamboozled into playing with her too.

Once we got settled in the living room, as settled as one gets while repeatedly throwing a ball to a retriever who can't stop, won't stop, it didn't take long for Sophia to shift the topic to my dating life.

"So, give me some updates!" she exclaimed. "Try to take my mind off of work and whatever this mystery ailment is that's been going on inside my body."

"Honestly, there's not much to tell. I haven't been on a date in a while, but I can give you some hospital gossip." I started petting Bowie in an effort to calm her down so I didn't have to play anymore.

"Oh? Yes, please! Give me the tea."

"You know what? You're actually getting better at using that lingo. It suits you when you're not trying so hard."

"Ashton, out with it!" She grew impatient.

"Well, apparently, there's a new guy there that a lot of the women have their eyes on. Even Kendal is crushing on him." I figured Kendal wouldn't mind me sharing that, since Sophia and her were besties and all.

"I don't remember this coming up in our girls group chat, but what's his name? Is he a doctor? A nurse? A respiratory therapist like you and Kendal?"

"I'm actually not sure of his position, and I haven't met him yet either. But there's word going around that he's a smokeshow, and the ladies are falling over themselves trying to get on the same assignments as him."

"Very exciting! I'll have to bring it up next time I talk to Kendal." She motioned for Bowie to come over and sit with her on the couch. "Is there anyone at work that you find attractive?"

"That place is filled with good-looking people, so, sure. But there's nobody I've made a connection with yet in that way since I've been there. I guess you could say I'm in a dry spell."

Wait. Where is something made out of wood? I need to knock on it. I can't just say something like that out loud and not knock on wood.

It registered that the coffee table was made of wood, so I knocked on the top of it three times, almost pleading with the universe to excuse my word choice.

"You'll meet someone," she said with confidence. "It's only a matter of time."

And somehow I knew she was right. I could almost feel the potential of a new love interest coming my way, but I didn't want it to be just anyone. I wanted it to be the right one.

"Are you getting excited about the joint birthday party for Owen and Bowie?" I asked my sister, covering Bowie's ears. I can't be spoiling the surprise for her.

"Yes! I can't wait. You made sure you have off from work, right?" she asked me, acting as if I was a rookie.

"Of course! I already got both Bowie and Mabel pink doggie floats for the pool. It'll be a sight to see!"

"Are you serious? Did you really just use the phrase, *a sight to see*? What's wrong with you?" Sophia asked, laughing at me. "Sounds to me like you've been hanging out with Mom and Dad too much."

"You're just jealous I thought of the float idea before you," I insisted. "I'm also making peanut butter cupcakes for them. Well, Owen can have some if he wants, since it's his party too. But you should probably check the ingredients and your list from the doctor before indulging."

"Got it! Ugh... I can see what potentially lies ahead for my diet, and I don't like it. But it is what it is, I guess."

6
———

SOPHIA

Celebrating Owen and Bowie at my parents' house was a lot of fun. Ashton left out the milk ingredient for the cupcakes, since I couldn't have dairy, so I was able to have one. And the dogs loved using their floats in the pool. They needed us to be in there with them, but once we were, they enjoyed relaxing and sunbathing. We ordered takeout food from one of Owen's favorite sandwich shops, played some card games, and sang to him and Bowie. Raelyn and Kevin even stopped by with Mr. and Mrs. Taylor. It was really a lovely day, and I was so thankful the weather cooperated.

Let's pray the same is true on our special day.

On another positive note, over the next couple of weeks, the wretched pain that sent me to the emergency room had faded away completely. I followed the diet religiously and took the meds as prescribed until they were gone, and eventually I was feeling back to normal.

Am I out of the woods? I sure hope so.

The wedding was just over a month away, and most

things had been taken care of, but I still had my final two dress fittings and my bachelorette party, which I had left completely up to the girls to plan. I knew I was in good hands because they all did a wonderful job with the bridal shower. The only downside was that Paityn was unable to be there because they couldn't travel to Pennsylvania twice in six weeks with how busy things were at work and Liam starting a new school year. She'd be at everything else though, and she very generously added to our honeymoon fund. Chloe was in the same boat and contributed to our trip as well.

Ireland, here we come!

Owen and I received everything we needed and more at the shower. Since we already lived together, we hadn't registered for as much as couples who were just starting out. Instead, we added the necessities for things that could use an upgrade, picked out some new bedding and toiletries, and created the fund for our European getaway as another option.

Other than that, we were just waiting to receive all of our invitation responses we had sent out a couple of weeks back so we would have an accurate count of who to expect. It was all coming together.

I used to dream about my wedding day when I was little. I always imagined what type of guy I would find and how he would propose. I would think about my dress and the veil and how the ceremony and reception would be covered in pink and purple flowers, maybe even some white. I used to practice dancing around in the living room to slow love songs, picturing myself having my first dance with my husband. Back then, I wasn't into country music, so it was always something by one of the boy bands I liked. And as perfect as everything looked in my mind, I somehow knew the reality would be better.

Suddenly, I was broken from my thoughts with the sound of a FaceTime call coming in from Paityn.

"Heyyy! What's going on? Miss me?" I asked her, answering the phone.

"Hey, hey! Of course, I do. We all do!" Paityn responded with a smile, Liam and bunny, Doug, beside her on the couch.

"Awww! How's my favorite nephew and his best buddy?" I directed my question at the snuggling that was almost too cute to witness.

"I'm the only nephew!" Liam exclaimed. He laughed and inched more into the screen to speak to me. "Doug misses Bowie. Can he come to the wedding?"

"Well, bud, I don't think we can have animals at the church, and Bowie is pretty sad about that too, but you can definitely bring Doug to stay over at Grandmom and Grandpop's house when you come here, and we will set up a play date!" I offered a compromise, knowing my parents wouldn't mind having Doug there.

"Yes! And Doug can play with Mabel too!" Liam said excitedly.

"Sounds like a plan! Are you ready to go back to school?" I asked, already knowing the answer. As much as Liam loved his classmates and teachers, I knew he enjoyed being home with Paityn, Bradley, and Doug so much more. His parents made him feel safe, since they knew him better than anyone, and having a therapy pet was known to be very calming for children with autism. Doug was also able to provide Liam with sensory support, which his pediatrician said he was in need of.

"I'm ready. I wish I could bring Doug sometimes, but we can't have a class pet," he responded with a pouty face.

"Yeah, they don't allow class pets at the schools here either, in case anyone is allergic or afraid. But I'm sure there are lots of fun things to do during the day in your classroom."

Liam gave me a partial smile and then leaned out of view to snuggle with Doug some more.

I don't blame him.

"So when do you have his first IEP meeting of the year? Do you know if he will have the same case manager and the same speech and language therapist?" I followed up with Paityn.

"He is going to have the same speech and language therapist, but I just found out his case manager is going to be different due to his new diagnosis. There is a meeting already scheduled for next week."

"That's great! It sounds like you are on top of everything, as usual. He's lucky to have you."

"Well, thank you. I try my best, and he has a lot of unique strengths, challenges, and needs, so I'm very fortunate to have the IEP team I do at his school. Of course, I couldn't do it without Brad either."

"Have there been any new behaviors you are seeing more frequently?" I asked, trying to learn more about the daily life of a seven-year-old diagnosed with autism.

"He's still exhibiting repetitive behaviors, like saying the same phrases over and over again, and he's still very sensitive to loud noises and certain textures, as well as not easily adapting to changes in his environment and routine, but I suppose the newest developments would be his executive functioning skills. According to his most recent evaluation,

Liam struggles with organization, planning, and problem solving. And I have seen it at home too."

"Interesting. What does the team or his pediatrician say is best to help with all of it?" I know a little about working with special education children from growing up with a mother who worked in the field, but it's different when the child is in your own family.

"The recommendations have been to redirect him when he is using the same statements and provide him with new and different terms and phrases, take him to or tell him to go to quiet places when the noises are too much for him or having him put on his noise canceling headphones, mixing in something out of his routine gradually, and giving him practice with organization whenever an opportunity presents itself. Another suggestion was to have Liam plan something once a week, whether it be a meal or an activity, and that seems to be going well. He loves when it's his turn to be in charge, and that also helps him with responsibility."

"Wow! I don't think I realized there was so much that went into accommodating a child on the spectrum and making sure he meets his goals." I had to give Paityn so much credit.

"It can be a lot, especially when he gets frustrated or anxious and has a meltdown, but he's worth it. I'd give him the world if I could," she replied, looking over at him with adoration. My eyes filled up at the sentiment.

"Liam couldn't have a better mother." I smiled and wiped the corners of my eyes with my hands. "And I couldn't have a better sister. I can't wait for all of you to be here for the wedding, and I'm so happy you will be standing next to me when I marry the love of my love."

"You're making me cry now! Stop it!" Paityn reached

for a tissue on the table nearby. "I'm counting down the days, Soph. And I'll try to be just as amazing as you were when you stood next to me on my wedding day."

Tears continued streaming down my face as I imagined myself walking down the aisle and standing at the altar.

I'm going to need tissues stuffed inside my dress!

7

ASHTON

Taylor Swift once said, "Being fearless is having a lot of fears, but you jump anyway." I interpreted this to mean that you move forward despite anxiety and apprehension. And I was ready to do just that.

The stretch of me having zero romantic prospects had possibly come to an end. I met a guy at the hospital last night on my shift who immediately caught my eye. We were paired up for rounds, and I was pleasantly surprised when I received my assignment. I had never seen him before and found out he had recently been hired. We clicked almost instantly, and the vibe was giving *we've met before in another life.*

Throughout the night, we talked about college and what made us want to work in the medical field. There wasn't any flirting. But I didn't know if that was because he was straight, taken, not interested, or simply just focused on his job. I didn't see a ring on his finger, so I assumed he wasn't married, unless he just didn't like wearing the ring. I made a mental note to try and find out more information about him without it being too obvious. I wasn't hiding the fact that I was bisexual anymore, but I wasn't screaming it from the rooftops either, especially not in a professional environment.

History had shown me that if I wanted someone to be comfortable with me, I had to be comfortable with myself. And I was. It took me a while, but I'd gotten there. I had accepted the person I'd become and was happy with that person. But that didn't mean the dating world became any easier for me. I still had a fear of rejection that a lot of people had when attempting to find their person. Even if you felt like someone was into you, you didn't always know to what degree or how long it would last or if they were into other people as well. And that became increasingly more difficult when you were a guy trying to initiate flirtatious dialogue with another guy without certainty they had the same sexual preference. I guess the same could be said when making the effort with a woman who might be fully gay.

All I could do was be myself and put myself out there, and whatever happened after that was meant to be. At least, I knew I wouldn't have regrets if I lived my life that way.

Let the pieces fall where they may.

THE ALERT CAME to my phone just as I was getting ready to take Mabel out for a walk.

> Kendal: Ashton James! Did you leave me on 'opened' last night?

If anyone close to me should know how busy things got at work, it was Kendal. And I sort of had other things on my mind that were more important than responding to a Snapchat message.

> Me: Hey, Kendal. Sorry about that. Work distractions. You know how it is.
> What's up?
>
> Kendal: Can you give me a ride to the hospital later? My car is being worked on. I saw we both have a 7am to 7pm shift again. Please?
>
> Me: Sure. I'll pick you up around 6:30. See you then!
>
> Kendal: Great! Thanks so much, Ash!

I gave a thumbs up on her last text and then hooked Mabel on to her leash. I had less than an hour before having to get ready to head back to work, but I wouldn't choose to spend my time any other way. On our walk, I told Mabel all about my new crush. She wagged her tail intently at each detailed description of his ruggedly handsome appearance as if she were staring at him herself. And maybe she would someday, if any of the odds were in my favor.

Okay, not me getting way ahead of myself.

"Hey, you better keep this to yourself, girl. Sophia will be jealous that I confided in a puppy first instead of her," I joked with Mabel as she padded along next to me. And she would really be fired up if she found out I talked to Kendal about it before her too, which was what I intended to do as soon as she got in my car. Kendal was a talker, and she somehow regularly had the scoop on everything. There was no way I wasn't asking her about the hot nurse.

I picked Kendal up out front of her house, and I gave her about five minutes of her own hospital gossip before I broke in with my inquiries about the mystery employee I couldn't stop thinking about.

"Do you know the new guy on staff, the tall, dark, and handsome one?" I asked her, hiding nothing.

"You mean you finally saw him?" she quickly responded.

"Him? How do you know who I'm talking about? There can be more than one new guy at work." Suddenly, I remembered her mentioning something about a guy she found appealing that had recently been employed.

"Is he a nurse? I only know of one new male nurse, as far as starting this summer anyway. It's the one I was telling you about before!"

"Yes, he's a nurse." And at the same time, both of us said his name.

"Sidney?!" We glanced at each other with wide eyes.

"Have you met him?" I asked without missing a beat.

"I've been on the same assignment with him a couple of times. He's really nice. Have you talked to him, Ash?"

"Last night was the first time I worked with him. I feel like maybe I saw him once before from a distance, but I was never close enough to introduce myself. He's really cool. Do you know anything about him?"

Kendal nonchalantly replied with what she knew I was dying to hear, "I know that he's single, if that's what you mean." And then she checked her makeup in the visor mirror.

"Do you know that for a fact? Or are you just inferring from conversation?"

"Sidney said he had just moved to the area, and I asked him if he had a roommate or a significant other to go out with and do things with when he wasn't at the hospital. That's when he told me he was flying solo."

"Interesting. So, what's your take on him?" I kept my eyes on the road, but I could feel Kendal staring at me from the passenger seat.

"My take? I told you, he's nice. And we both know he's good-looking," she said with certainty, not understanding what I was getting at.

"No, I mean... did you get any vibes from him?"

"Vibes? Oh... you mean, like gay vibes? Honestly, I wasn't even thinking about it, and nothing really stands out, but that doesn't mean he isn't. God, I hope he's straight!"

"Wow... okay, so you're into him too. That's a first." I never thought I'd be in competition with one of my sister's best friends for a potential date.

"This is funny," Kendal said as we parked in the employee lot. "You shoot your shot, and I'll shoot mine?" She laughed, getting out of my car and shutting the door.

I let out a long sigh and joined her, locking up with my key. "Don't let this cause a problem for us, okay?" I kindly requested. Her wild side made me nervous sometimes.

"Of course, not! It's all in good fun." She tickled me at my waist and laughed some more.

It's all fun and games until someone gets hurt.

THROUGHOUT MY SHIFT, all I could think about was how no good could come from Kendal and I going after the same guy. I loved her like a sister, just the same way I loved Raelyn. And we worked together. I didn't want anything to ruin the relationship we had. We both needed to tread lightly and then agree to be okay with defeat.

There were a few ways the whole thing could go. One was that Sidney preferred women and would decide to explore things with Kendal. Another was that he was gay and would possibly give me a chance. The third option was that he wouldn't have interest in either of us. And that would be a shame, but at least there wouldn't be conflict with Kendal over which one of us he was spending time with. Well, and I guess there's another way this could go too. Sidney could be interested in both men and women, just like me, and he could want to see where things go with both of us.

"Hey, I meant to ask you earlier," I said to Kendal when I saw her in passing hours later. "Are you bringing a date to Sophia and Owen's wedding?"

"Since I'm a bridesmaid and all, I thought I'd go stag. I'll be busy with bridal activities and don't want some poor guy to have to fend for himself when I'm not around."

"Yeah, I get that. Besides, you'll have an opportunity to mingle if you go single, am I right?" I joked, but I was seriously hoping she would meet someone at my sister's wedding and then lose interest completely in our new nurse.

"Ashton James, are you trying to take me out of the equation so soon?" Kendal replied with a smirk. "I could mingle at the wedding and still exert effort here. Can't put all my eggs in one basket!"

"True, true, very true. Well, I'm not bringing anyone either. I also didn't want a date to feel lonely with me being in the wedding like you, but I didn't really have anyone I wanted to take. If only I had met Sidney sooner."

"You wish, buddy!" She flipped her hair with her right hand and smiled confidently. "I saw him first! But you can dream."

I will, Kendal, I definitely will.

We both had a laugh and bumped fists before going off on our separate ways.

8

SOPHIA

Preparing for a wedding evoked a myriad of emotions, and my nerves had taken center stage amid a symphony of feelings. As the big day approached, a mixture of excitement, anticipation, and anxiety intertwined, creating a jittery sensation I could barely tolerate. The seamstress at the bridal shop practically yelled at me for losing more weight and made me promise her to eat a couple of hamburgers in the days leading up to the nuptials in order to ensure my dress would fit.

Every detail seemed to carry the weight of a thousand expectations. The desire for perfection, coupled with the fear of unforeseen mishaps, was sending pulses of uneasiness through my entire body. But with it, came an undercurrent of joy and love in getting to marry my best friend and soulmate.

Owen was everything. And I know a lot of people say that about the person they are about to marry, but it was true. He was. He was caring and kind, and he was thoughtful and understanding. He was clever and funny. And mostly, he loved me.

I was about to marry the man of my dreams, the person that stood out way above and beyond every other man I'd ever even spoken to in my life. And it was happening on this day, in front of everyone we both loved. Owen Taylor was going to be my husband, and Raelyn was going to my sister-in-law. No other scenario could have played out more perfectly than this one.

"Are you ready to do this?" I heard a voice behind me say as I was fixing my veil in the mirror on top of my flowy curls and around my shoulders. It was the voice I needed to hear in that moment, my stomach feeling like there were a hundred butterflies taking flight.

"I think I am, Rae." Tears filled my eyes, and I took a deep breath, in slowly and out even slower.

Stop it, Sophia. You'll ruin your fabulously applied makeup.

"You got this, girl. Or should I say sis?" Raelyn smiled and dabbed at my eyes with a tissue she pulled from the box on a nearby table in the bridal suite.

"I can't believe I get to call you my sister today." I held the tears back and put on my very happy bride face. "How do I look?"

Raelyn stared at me with the admiration that only a true friend who was about to actually become family could give. "You look like you're about to make my brother completely lose it on the altar."

She and I held a warm embrace, and then I made my way toward the door, knowing everyone was waiting to get the show on the road. When I stepped out into the vestibule of the church, my dad was standing there with an arm out, ready to walk me down the aisle. I latched my left arm into his right and took another deep breath. Raelyn joined Paityn, Kendal, Bethany, and Hope in front of me, along with Liam, who was ready to fulfill his ring bearer duties, and the music began to play. My chest tightened, and my heart swelled as I fought to keep it together.

I stared down at the entire wedding party standing in place at the altar. Mere minutes were all that were left. I was about to become Mrs. Owen Taylor, a title I had dreamt of for so many years. My dad looked at me, telling me with his eyes that it was time to walk, that he was ready to give me away, even though I would always be a daddy's girl.

"Okay, Dad. Let's do this," I whispered to him as I took my first step.

"Just smile until you reach Owen," he whispered back. "It will stop you from crying." He knew me all too well.

I followed his advice and held a soft smile as I made eye contact with our guests, gliding down the center of the church, Dad holding on tightly.

As I approached Owen, I saw his eyes welling up. I guess Raelyn was right. Either that, or he was feeling all of the same emotions I was.

The ceremony proceeded with grace, punctuated by prayers, readings, and our traditional vows to each other. The priest's voice resonated through the church as he spoke words of wisdom and guidance, uniting us together until death do us part.

After exchanging rings and a spectacular kiss that couldn't have been better if we had rehearsed it, we turned toward our guests, their faces radiant with happiness. Applause filled the church as we walked hand in hand back down the aisle, now husband and wife, ready to embark on our journey together.

THE WEDDING RECEPTION was held in a large ballroom with shimmering lights. Round tables draped in crisp white linens were elegantly arranged, each adorned with centerpieces of candles and delicate blooms that added a touch of romance to the atmosphere.

The dance floor beckoned as the lead singer of the band sang All of Me by John Legend, the song that brought us our first kiss on our very first date. What else would we have chosen as our wedding song? It was *our* song, with only one other a close second - Shallow by Bradley Cooper and Lady Gaga.

At our sweetheart table, Owen and I sat, beaming with the realization that we had tied the knot. My gown, now bustling with intricate folds and pins, sparkled under the soft glow of the chandeliers above. Owen, oh-so-dapper in his tailored suit, couldn't take his eyes off me, his hand gently resting on mine through each course of the meal.

The reception continued to unfold seamlessly, as our family and friends prepared to deliver their speeches. And the funniest part of the night was brought to us by Raelyn and Kendal, who performed a rap duet that delved deep into the history of my relationship with Owen and ended with a joke about how my life had drastically improved by becoming a member of the Taylor family. After gaining another sister, who was already my best friend, and marrying the most incredible guy on the planet, I was apt to agree.

But the speeches that brought tears to both my eyes and to Owen's were the ones given by Paityn and Kevin. Paityn was my obvious choice for matron of honor, and Kev was chosen because he was the closest guy in Owen's life, other than his father. The best man speech was first.

Kevin stood tall holding the mic without an ounce of

discomfort or nervousness, seemingly at ease in front of the crowd. "Good evening, everyone! For those of you who don't know me, I'm Kevin, the best man and the proud brother-in-law of our handsome groom, and I'd love to share a few words. First off, let's all take a moment to appreciate how stunning Sophia looks in her dress. Owen, you're one lucky man!"

A smattering of applause bounced around the room and a hearty whoop could be heard from the back, making me blush.

Kevin chuckled and continued, "From the moment I first met Sophia many years ago as my wife's best friend, I knew she was someone special. And the way she lights up even more when she is with Owen, knowing how much they love and support each other, is truly remarkable. I would say that it's inspiring, but I like to believe Raelyn and I inspired these two to find their happily ever after!"

A few chuckles were heard throughout the room. "Now, this is a day of celebration for the wonderful life they are about to begin in unity. Remember that marriage is about partnership and understanding, two things they seem to have mastered, but it's also about finding joy in the little moments and being adventurous when the opportunities come. Let's raise our glasses to Owen and Sophia! Here's to a lifetime of memories and an endless love that will only get stronger with time!"

Owen quickly dabbed his eyes with his handkerchief and then shared it with me. Tears had already begun streaming down my face, and we couldn't have my makeup ruined completely, with another speech on the heels of Kevin's.

"Good evening to all of you!" My sister said as she took the microphone. "I'm Paityn, the matron of honor, and more importantly, the proud older sister of the beautiful bride. Growing up with Sophia was one of the greatest gifts of my life. We've shared things only two sisters as close as the two of us could, from childhood escapades to teenage drama to deep conversations as we got older. And I wouldn't trade one minute of it for anything in the world."

She took a pause and then began to speak again. "I knew about Sophia's love for Owen before he did, and maybe even before she realized it herself. Friends don't talk about each other the way she talked about him. And I knew she'd eventually have to confess. Otherwise, she'd have gone crazy with regrets of what could've been. Thankfully, she doesn't have to. Her love was made known, and it was requited, and here we are today, celebrating that love."

Paityn looked at me with wet eyes. "Owen, you not only won her heart, but you've won the hearts of our entire family, and we are blessed to officially welcome you into it with open arms and our full support. Sophia, you've always been my rock, and I know you'll always be Owen's too. But please let him be yours, just as you've allowed me to steady you over the years." She held her glass filled halfway with champagne in the air. "Let's toast to a couple that was written in the stars and was always meant to find their way to everlasting enchantment together!"

I took a sip from my own glass and then immediately stood up to welcome my sister in for a hug.

Where is that handkerchief?

AS DINNER WAS SERVED, the aroma of the gourmet dishes we selected filled the room, and the steak, chicken, and seafood options were paired with fine wines. Candles flickered on the tables, casting a warm ambiance that encouraged intimate conversations and shared memories among our guests.

Throughout the night, the celebration continued with the cutting of the cake, the tossing of the bouquet, and the lively beat of the music that kept everyone on their feet. From the youngest children to the oldest relatives, all joined in the festivities, creating a sense of unity and love that permeated every corner of the ballroom. And at the center of the group of children in attendance, were my adorable niece and nephew.

"Hope!" I heard Liam shout over the music as I approached them. "I forgot to tell you that Doug met Mabel! They play so good! I think they love each other!" he exclaimed.

"Can I watch them play?" Hope asked with excitement in her voice.

"Of course you can. I'll tell Mommy to tell Uncle Eli to bring you over."

"Yay!" She responded, cute and cheerfully, clapping her hands together gently. I couldn't get over how completely obsessed I was with the two of them, and I was convinced that being an aunt was probably the best job in the world.

"I heard it was a very nice introduction, Liam," I chimed in. "I would love to see them have a playdate too."

Hope smiled, and Liam clung tightly to me, hugging my gown as I swayed back and forth with them to the music before excusing myself for a much needed drink refill.

While I was standing at the bar, Ashton and Rae appeared on each side of me, Kendal following close behind them.

"Can you believe I caught the bouquet?" Kendal asked

Ashton. "What do you think this means?" she smirked and elbowed my baby brother.

"It probably means you have good eye-hand coordination, I think," he replied, snapping right back at her. "Don't get any ideas in your head."

"Too late for that, buddy! I have big plans!" she said with a laugh.

"Okay, I feel like I'm missing something here. Does somebody want to tell me what's going on?" I smiled and looked at Rae for help. She shrugged her shoulders. Clearly, she was just as confused as I was.

"What's going on is Kendal's getting a little ahead of herself," Ashton said with a slight cockiness in his tone.

"I need more information. Are you guys playing some kind of game here at the wedding?" I asked, glancing around the room at eligible bachelors and bachelorettes.

"We are definitely not playing a game, and whatever is happening isn't happening here. Just forget it!" Kendal told me, signaling for the bartender to get us all a round.

"But there is something happening? Yes?" I raised an eyebrow.

"There is really nothing happening," Ashton said calmly. "We're just messing with each other. There's nothing for you to worry about. This is your day!" He retrieved the drinks that were placed on the bar moments earlier and handed one to each of us before picking up his own. "To Sophia and Owen! May your troubles be few and your blessings be many."

"Wow! Look at you throwing in an Irish blessing to tie the wedding and honeymoon together!" I raised my glass in delight.

We clinked our glasses together, drank to that beautiful

sentiment, and danced the rest of the night away, wishing it would never end.

———

LESS THAN THREE DAYS LATER, Owen and I arrived at our hotel in the Emerald Isle. Our trip included two nights in Dublin, three nights in Wicklow, and then two nights over in Liscannor. We rented a car to drive to the other locations but then had to return back to Dublin on the last day and fly home from there.

We checked into The Maldron in Dublin and then did a bit of sightseeing, since our room wasn't quite ready. St. Patrick's Cathedral was a block from where we were staying, so that was our first stop. Then we headed over to Our Lady of Mount Carmel Church.

"We should go into one of the libraries," I suggested, as we were walking through town. "William Butler Yeats is my favorite poet!"

"I see one on that street to the right," he said, pointing in that direction.

We entered Marsh's Library and received a very nice tour that led us to a chair that James Joyce once sat in to do a reading of his work. I couldn't help myself from sitting in the chair and asking Owen to photograph me.

How could I not?

From there, we found our way back to the hotel, had a quick nap, and then got ourselves ready for our first dinner abroad. And when I say it was the best food I'd ever had in my life, I was not exaggerating. We landed at a restaurant a few blocks in walking distance and tried a variety of menu options, from beers to appetizers to entrees to desserts. And our server even brought over some Baby Guinness drinks for us to try.

More please!

When we woke up the next morning, Owen was excited to take a walk around the city and perhaps do some shopping or visit an old castle. There really was so much to see in so little time. And I needed to get to the Jameson Distillery too. Elijah had asked me to pick him up a legit bottle of whiskey from there, and there was no way I was letting him down.

We ended up doing all of the things on our list and had the best time trying different whiskey drinks. I even became a new fan of Jameson. We secured a gift for Elijah, as well as for all of our other family members at a cute shop nearby, and then wandered into an old Irish pub for some dinner. They had live music, bagpipes included, and I felt I was having the true Ireland experience. Owen's favorite part of the meal was listening to our waiter speak with his heavy accent.

I can't wait to see what more of this country is like!

The next day, we checked out, got in our rental car, and drove to Wicklow. After getting settled at a bed and breakfast, Owen and I drove to Powerscourt Estate, which was named to be the third best garden in the world by National Geographic. I had read about it online and immediately added it to our itinerary. It had forty-seven acres to explore and get lost in, and we were up for the challenge.

"Look, there's a swan over there!" I said as we were walking by an expansive pond filled with lily pads and lotus.

"Wow! So cool! I'll take some photos," Owen said, focusing his lens.

"I heard we're not supposed to get too close though.

They can be aggressive and mean when trying to protect their territory or their nests," I added, taking in the beauty while I spoke.

"No worries! We will just admire from afar and be on our way," he said.

We spent two hours walking through the estate, enjoying the sunshine and cool breeze and taking pictures of the flowers and of each other. I personally could have spent the entire day there, but we knew of a waterfall we were eager to see.

"Owen, that's incredible!" I exclaimed when we were in view. "The website did not do this justice."

"Imagine living in a town like this, where you could spend a part of your day anytime you wish just watching and listening to this breath-taking waterfall." He stared at it as if it were the most fascinating piece of nature he'd ever laid eyes on. And that said a lot, considering all we have seen as photographers.

"We are definitely coming back here tomorrow," I insisted.

"I don't need any convincing, Soph. I've never looked at anything more stunning, except for you."

And we returned the following day after spending some time at the distillery on the same property. But it was like we were there for the first time. That's how captivating it felt.

"We made the right choice for our honeymoon," I said as we began to stroll away from the extravagant cascade.

It was true too. This country was magical and so full of adventure and romance. I'd never forget the memories I was making with Owen here.

FOR THE LAST couple of days of our honeymoon, we stayed in Liscannor, a village very close to the famous Cliffs of Moher, which was a major bucket list item for both of us. As soon as we settled our luggage inside our small cottage and refreshed ourselves for the day, we grabbed an early lunch and headed straight for the cliffs.

For the second time in a week, I was left speechless. The landscape was alive with motion, seabirds wheeling and diving along the rockface, waves crashing below. Being here felt like standing on the edge of the world, powerful, humbling, and soul-stirring. The sight of sheep grazing peacefully on nearby fields was a quiet reminder of the everyday life that continued alongside such dramatic natural beauty.

"Sophia, lay down right here on your side," Owen directed me, pointing to a grassy space a few feet from the edge. "I never want to forget this moment." He got his camera ready as I positioned myself.

"Make sure you post this one on our socials when we get back home," I said with a smile, trying to look as comfortable as possible. "I'll look so brave and carefree!"

"Oh, baby, this is getting posted everywhere and put in a frame," he replied, removing the camera from his face to take it all in. "I can't believe I get to call you my wife."

I stood up cautiously and approached him, arms stretched out in front of me, ready for a warm embrace. He brought me in, kissing my lips as I fell against him. And in that moment, wrapped in his arms, I felt whole.

9

ASHTON

Sophia and Owen's wedding was the best I'd ever been to. Maybe that was because it was the only wedding I'd ever been in as a groomsman, or maybe it was because my sister just looked so happy and so in love. Either way, I would relive that whole day and night if I could. The only change I would have made is for me to have had a romantic plus-one by my side.

It seemed like Kendal did her fair share of mingling at the reception, but for me, it was more difficult. And not because I was bisexual, but more because I already knew nearly everyone my age there, and the few I didn't were just dates of people I did. There was one girl there who caught my eye, someone who resembled Owen's family, so I could only assume she was a cousin of his. We were up at the bar at the same time twice, and I smiled at her the first time when she made eye contact. The second time, she actually took the initiative and asked if I needed a drink as she was ordering. I accepted and thanked her, attempting to have further dialogue. She was very cute and appeared to be about mid-twenties, but when I was about to ask her for her name, the DJ announced another part of the evening, and we made our way back to our designated tables. I supposed it wasn't meant to be, and if it were, then we would cross paths again at some point in the future. Owen was my family now, after all. And I had to just keep the faith that what was meant for me would simply come to find me when the time was right.

Speaking of interests though, I was hoping to continue getting to know Sidney. There hadn't been another shift where I was on the same assignments since the one and only night when I'd met him and we talked so easily. Kendal had had a few, so I figured I was due for one soon. I knew she was planning on feeling things out with him, so I had to do the same. Though I definitely picked up on an energy between us, I had learned from the past that I could never be too sure. I had to keep it real and ask the right questions. The worst thing to happen would be for him to either not be into guys or not be into me, and I would then be in the same position I was now.

I have nothing to lose.

"HEY, you! How's my favorite little brother?" Kendal asked as she approached the schedule board at the hospital. I had just gotten there myself and was looking to see who I'd be with.

"What's up? I'm good, and you?"

She and I had a shift together at least once a week. I was starting to see more of her than I did Sophia, so it made sense that she had evolved to calling me her little brother. Kendal didn't have any siblings, and I was happy to fill that role if she needed me to. I just hoped this whole thing with Sidney didn't mess that up.

"I'm great! And you are a lucky duck! You're working with Sidney for our first few hours. Keep your hands to yourself, okay?" She laughed and playfully nudged me in the shoulder.

"Right, yeah, because you have to worry about me being too assertive." I held in my excitement, but I was pretty confident Kendal could tell I was elated about having the chance to spend time with our mutual crush.

"Listen, all jokes aside, you should put your best foot forward. There's a real possibility Sidney is gay and very much attracted to you and not me. And that would be totally fine!"

"And the opposite may be true too, so we'll see what happens. Neither of us resents the other though. Deal?" I felt better knowing how cool she was being about it.

"Ashton, bet!"

"Ugh. First Sophia, and now her. Just say the word 'deal'. You guys sound ridiculous." I laughed and hustled out to start my shift.

IN THE BUSTLING corridors of Doylestown Hospital, the air was filled with the sterile scent of disinfectant and the low hum of medical equipment. Amidst the controlled chaos, Sidney and I found ourselves at the nurses' station, our banter a playful respite from the night's demands.

"You know," I teased, tapping my pen against the clipboard, "I heard another one of our colleagues talking about you earlier. Rumor has it there is a new patient on the third floor who's asking for you by name."

Sidney chuckled, a dimpled smile spreading across his face. "Ah, my adoring fans. I'll try to squeeze them in if I can."

I raised an eyebrow, my gaze lingering on his mouth. "Or maybe they just heard you've got the best... bedside manner?"

Sidney laughed, shaking his head. "Well, someone has to make sure our patients feel appreciated."

Our conversation was suddenly interrupted by a call on the intercom, summoning both of us to the ICU.

I sighed, gathering my things. "Duty calls. But maybe later we can continue discussing your special skills."

Did I really say that out loud? Wow.

Sidney grinned, holding up his right first for me to bump before we both began making our way to the elevator. "Count on it."

Was that a flirty fist bump? A friendly one? Just two coworkers ending dialogue? Why am I so bad at this?

Hours later, during a brief lull in our long shift, I found myself in the break room, finally able to catch my breath. Sidney entered with two cups of coffee, handing one to me with a smirk.

"Thought you could use a pick-me-up," he said, leaning against the counter.

I took a sip, my eyes meeting his over the rim of the cup. "You read my mind. Thank you so much."

Sidney smiled, breaking eye contact. "I try to be attentive to my coworkers' needs. That's all."

I set my cup down, stepping closer. "And what about your needs, Sid? Can I call you Sid?" I swallowed past the lump in my throat and spoke again. "What do you need?"

What has gotten into me?

Our proximity charged the air with a subtle tension, the hospital noises fading into the background.

"That's a good question. I'm so used to focusing on what everyone else needs, that I don't think about my needs too often. I guess it comes with the profession."

"I hear you. I'm very similar in that sense." There was a long pause between us, and I was worried it would get awkward and that he'd lose interest, so I mustered up some courage and kept it going. "If you could think of one thing I could do for you, what would it be?"

If this guy is straight, that came off super weird, but this is me, putting myself out there.

He put his right hand to his chin in a pondering motion and looked up to the ceiling. "I could really use a night out, and you seem like a cool person to go into town with, yeah? Would you show me the hot spots?"

What? Did he just ask me to hang out with him outside of work? Kendal will die.

The moment was interrupted by the buzz of our pagers, reminding us of the reality of our surroundings. We exchanged a knowing glance, the promise of more lingering between us.

———

THE NIGHT CAME to go out into town with Sidney. I was stoked to have some time with him off the clock and away from any emergencies that usually arose at the hospital. I wore a button down shirt with jeans and a pair of Hey Dudes to complete the outfit. In retrospect, I should've worn socks, given how sweaty the thought of being alone with him made me, but it was too late. I had parked down the street from a few well-known bars in the area and was walking up the sidewalk to begin what I hoped to be the first of many outings with an amazing guy.

When I saw him standing outside, waiting for me to arrive, I couldn't take my eyes off of him.

Look away, Ashton. Don't be creepy.

And he watched me approach him every step of the way.

That has to mean he's interested, right?

I shook his hand and then guided him toward a place called Chambers. They always had live music, and right next door was a place called The Other Side. It was the other side of Chambers.

Clever. I know.

The bar was dimly lit, brimming with chatter and the sounds of an 80's cover band, people singing along to every word. We found two seats along the bar, and I ordered the first round of beers, which was only fair considering the last time we were together, he bought me a coffee.

"Cheers to new colleagues and new friends?" Sidney proposed as he raised his glass in the air.

Friends? I hope to be more.

I didn't respond verbally. Instead, I smiled and raised my glass up and then took a sip, maintaining eye contact, of course, because it was bad luck if you didn't.

"What do you like to do in your spare time when you're not working?" I asked him, fighting to chat over the music.

"You mean aside from this?" Sidney chuckled and drank more of his beer. "I don't know really. I guess I like going to concerts, movies, and good restaurants. But I also love just hanging in sometimes too, ya know? I like to read and do puzzles. Don't judge."

"No judgment here! I love puzzles, especially when I get to do them with my nephew and niece. Although, I'm sure the puzzles you do are a lot more of a time investment. It doesn't take hours to put together one with forty pieces." I chuckled. Conversation felt so easy with him. "And I love live music too, which is why I wanted to come here." I gestured over at the band.

"Well, I'm sure Uncle Ashton has some fun with those puzzles!" He returned the laugh, which I greatly appreciated. "How about food? Do you like going out, or do you prefer to stay in and cook?"

I like that it's not just me asking the questions.

"I do have fun, but I'd be open to trying bigger and better if you have a puzzle you need some assistance on," I threw him a flirty smirk. "And I like both eating in and going out, depending on my mood."

"I might take you up on that offer sometime soon, if you think you can keep up," Sidney replied. "And if you tried my cooking, you'd want to eat in more often."

Is he saying he wants to cook for me? Am I blushing?

I put the back sides of my hands to my cheeks to cool my face. I didn't feel warm. Thank God.

"Did it just get hot in here?" he asked, basically reading my mind. Then he smiled as he slowly slid out of his stool. "Want to check out what's going on next door?"

"Sure, let's go!" I told him, almost too eagerly.

We finished the rest of our beers and then walked over to The Other Side. A sensation that I'd never really felt before rushed through my body, like I was getting really close to having exactly what I wanted.

And then...

What the hell?! What is she doing here?

"Ash! Hey! You know Emily, right?" Kendal lightly shoved a blonde woman in front of her who looked vaguely familiar. "She's a nurse at the hospital."

"I think we've been on some shifts together, yes," I looked suspiciously at Kendal.

What is she up to?

"We definitely have," Emily responded. "Hey, Sid!" She leaned in to hug Sidney, who was standing to the right side of me. "Glad we found you!"

Found him? Why were they looking for him?

"Me too! It's so crowded that I wasn't sure you would. Ashton really does know where the hot spots are." Sidney smiled in my direction.

So much for me getting to know him one-on-one tonight.

"Well, he has his older sister and her two super cool besties to thank for that! We showed him the nightlife here in D-town." Kendal laughed and then locked eyes with Sidney, a little too long.

"Right, yes, so, it's a party now that you're here," I raised my beer in Kendal's direction. "You guys getting a drink?"

"Oh, for sure! Do you two need anything? My treat!" Emily offered, and we told her what we were drinking.

"I hope you don't mind that I told Emily and Kendal we were heading out tonight. I mentioned Chambers but wasn't sure if they would come." Sidney whispered to me while Emily and Kendal were ordering from the bartender.

"It's okay with me. Kendal and I are almost family, so I'm used to being around her. And Emily is super sweet."

But I still wasn't sure why they had to be *here*? Was she seriously trying to hijack my night? I'd thought we said we'd play nice and this… just didn't seem to be sportsman-like, if you asked me.

"That's right, you two know each other outside of work. Is she as cool as she seems?"

Is he trying to get information on Kendal? Does he like her? Ugh.

"She's really cool, yeah. My sister says she's a wild child, but that's one of her best friends, so I guess, she's a good time."

Maybe Sidney likes wild? Or, maybe he doesn't?

"Noted." He took the final sip of his beer just before Emily and Kendal returned with fresh ones.

For the next hour, the conversation went back and forth between the four of us. There was some friendly banter and some flirty banter, but oddly enough, some of the flirty banter was happening between myself and Emily. I wasn't sure if Kendal had put Emily up to it or if she was genuinely interested, but it seemed like she was trying to get to know me. I found I was dividing my attention between the two nurses, both of whom were very attractive, and Sidney was dividing his attention between myself and Kendal.

I was feeling both delighted at the idea of having two potential prospects and confused at what type of person Sidney was actually into. It appeared he liked me, but it also appeared he was captivated by Kendal. She was beautiful, don't get me wrong, but he couldn't have both of us. In this particular scenario, he most certainly could not have his cake and eat it too.

10

SOPHIA

An entire week away completely off the grid with my favorite person almost made me forget about my upcoming appointment with the gastroen-terologist. It had been scheduled for the middle of October, and that day was swiftly approaching. Owen and my parents had offered to go with me to see the doctor, but ulti-mately, I decided I wanted to go and do it alone. I figured if there were next steps that had to be followed, they could help me take it from there.

I showed up at the office fifteen minutes prior to my appointment time, just like I was told, so that I could fill out any necessary paperwork. The receptionist handed me a clipboard and asked me to have a seat, assuring me they would be calling me back momentarily. While I was wait-ing, various scenarios ran through my head of what could have caused me to end up in the emergency room, and this wasn't the first time I let my imagination run wild. But at least, this time, I was about to speak with a doctor who specialized in all issues pertaining to the colon, and I could ask any questions I had.

"Sophia James?" I heard a woman call my name out.

"Yes, that's me." I stood up, gathering my things, and followed her back to the gastroenterologist's room.

The nurse made her exit shortly after dropping me off, closing the door behind her. The doctor greeted me with a handshake, introducing himself.

"Sophia, it's nice to meet you. I'm Doctor Yang. Please, have a seat." While making his way to the chair at his desk, he motioned with his hand for me to take the chair on the opposite side. "I understand you suffered some heavy pain alongside your abdomen. Is that correct?" He looked at his computer screen briefly, which I assumed was my report from the day I had gone into the hospital.

"Yes, I did. I wasn't sure if it was something I had eaten or if I had some type of infection or even something worse. It was pretty scary. It still is, if I'm being straightforward."

"I completely understand why it was concerning then and why it is now. Our health is serious, and not knowing what's causing a problem can be extremely stressful. But we will get to the bottom of it." I noticed a slight smile begin to spread on his face, and then he struck back to professional mode. "The conclusion made by the emergency room physician was inflammation of the colon. As you may know, this can be caused by specific food intake, celiac disease, irritable bowel syndrome, colitis, the development of Crohn's disease, and reduced blood flow."

Everything Doctor Yang was saying, I had read online, but it was different hearing it from him. It somehow seemed more real and possible and not just a problem that another person may have had. Instead of looking at statistics, I was facing the reality that I could be a statistic.

"I'm sending you home with a list of dietary restrictions, as well as a script for Quest Diagnostics. I want you to go to the nearest location over this next week and have them run a celiac test for you. I don't think that's what is going on here, but I'd like to rule it out first."

"I understand. I will get that taken care of right away." I took the list of food and drinks that I have to stay away from and the script for the celiac testing and put them both in my purse.

"And I'd like to do a colonoscopy sometime before the end of the calendar year. Usually the procedure is first completed around the age of forty-five, but given the circumstances, we should begin the process as soon as possible." A very large knot formed in my stomach, and I could feel my eyes filling up. "I can see this is difficult to take in, but I assure you we will walk you through every step and answer any questions you may have."

I held myself together by taking some deep breaths and reminding myself to not worry until I had to. I didn't like the idea of having to get an IV put in and having to be put to sleep, but something about this doctor made me trust that I would get through it. "Alright, I will schedule it for December before the craziness of the holidays commences." I left his office and went to the room next door to make the appointment.

I still have several weeks to mentally prepare.

WHEN I GOT HOME, both Owen and Bowie were waiting for me in the living room. I could tell Owen was stressed out from the way he was snuggled up with Bowie, using her for emotional support, just the way I'd done many times.

"Hey! How'd it go? Did you get any piece of mind?" he

asked, sitting up on the couch and releasing his grip from our furball.

"It went okay. I was anxious throughout the appointment, but the doctor was calming and informative. I have to get a celiac test done and a colonoscopy." I sat down on the couch to the right of him. He pulled me in for a long embrace, which was eventually interrupted by Bowie not wanting to be left out. "Are you Mommy's special girl?" I asked her as she climbed across Owen from the left side of the couch and onto my lap.

She is getting way too big for this.

"When do you have to do each of those? Did he say it was urgent?"

"The celiac test has to be done over the next week, but I was able to wait until December to have the colonoscopy. He wants to rule things out and take it step by step, and I have no choice but to follow doctor's orders."

"Well, if you find out it's celiac disease, will there still be a need for the colonoscopy? Is it better to have both done just to be safe?" Owen asked.

"We didn't talk about that, but I'm assuming it will still be necessary. Maybe I should've had you come with me. I feel like there are a bunch of things I should have asked him but didn't think to."

"Listen... we are going to get through this. We'll find out what's wrong and cross whatever bridge we have to if and when it comes to that." He softly kissed me on the cheek, rubbing my back simultaneously.

"Thank you for the *we*. It makes me feel better knowing I'm not alone."

"It's always *we* from now on. You're my wife! Remember?" Owen said with a sweet tone in his voice.

"I sure do love the sound of that, husband." I tilted my head to rest on his shoulder.

Maybe we can focus on this married life thing instead.

"How about we get out of here and go to our happy place? I'll run and grab Bowie's leash and put her in my truck."

"Perfect! Do you mind if I invite Ashton? He loves going to the lake with Mabel, and he wanted to know how things went with the doctor too."

"Fine with me. Give him a call." He riled Bowie up for the outing while I got my brother on the phone. I loved how Owen always knew exactly what I needed.

PEACE VALLEY PARK had become my favorite place to go over the last few years. And it's not just because Owen and I have had so many great days and nights there, leading to many great memories. There was something so calming about being in or around Lake Galena. Whether I was kayaking or in a canoe or walking with the water in my sights, it somehow made my worries fade away for a while. And I was starting to think it had the same effect on Ashton. He was a regular now, as was Mabel, and when all of us were there together, it was very comforting.

We arrived in the parking lot just as my brother was helping Mabel out of his car. Bowie was so excited to see both of them, she nearly pulled my arm out of its socket trying to get over there.

"Relax, girl. I don't need another reason to go to the hospital. Sheesh!" I said to her, though she showed no signs of slowing.

Nobody knew Ashton better than I did, and I could tell

within the first five minutes together that something was up. So I took the first chance I had to crack that case wide open.

"How's work been, Ash?" I started there, knowing his jobs could be stressful at times.

"Work is fine, I guess. I don't know. I'm feeling exhausted lately. I'm not sure I can keep up with both jobs for much longer." He bent down to untangle Mabel's leash as it was getting wrapped around her legs.

"I didn't want to say anything, but you do look a little tired."

Why do I get the sense that's not all that is bothering him?

"Yeah, thanks," he chuckled lightly. "I might have to give the restaurant my notice, even though I'd hate to lose the extra cash. I take being a respiratory therapist seriously, and I really need to give it my all there."

"That's totally valid, and very responsible of you," I reassured him.

"You have to do what you have to do!" Owen chimed in.

"I appreciate it, guys." Ashton stared out at the lake as we continued to walk the girls on the path.

"What else is going on?" I asked, attempting to break him from his thoughts.

"Well..." He hesitated for a moment, showing he was uncertain how to talk about it. "There's this situation with Kendal, but I don't want you to be in the middle of it."

"Kendal? What situation? Did something happen at work? She hasn't said anything."

It was hard for me to believe Kendal and Ashton could have a conflict. Kendal loved Ashton like a little brother.

"It has to do with work, sort of, but it didn't happen there. It was when we were out the other night," he responded vaguely.

"You and her went out together? Where did you go? And why didn't I get an invite?" she joked.

"You were still on your honeymoon, and we didn't go out together. I went out with a guy from work, but Kendal and another nurse kinda showed up where we were. And, well, things got weird."

"Oh, right. Well, I need more details. So, there were four of you hanging out? Who was the guy?" Bowie tugged on the leash again, but thankfully this time, Owen took the loop off my wrist and slid it onto his own, allowing me to give my undivided attention to Ashton's juicy story.

"Since you were occupied with the wedding and getting ready for the honeymoon, and I've been busy with both jobs, I haven't really had a good chance to fill you in, but basically Kendal and I like the same guy at the hospital. His name is Sidney, and he's a nurse. And I made plans to go out in town with him over this past weekend."

I stopped walking and put my hands up. "Wait... Kendal likes a guy who is gay, a guy who you are interested in? Does she know he's gay? That doesn't make any sense."

"The thing is that neither of us knows if he is gay or not. It remains to be seen. He is super friendly with both of us, and he hasn't done anything that would confirm any preferences he has."

"So the two of you are just trying to see who he's into? And that's not a problem?"

Ashton told us all about the deal he made with Kendal regarding Sidney and how the two of them agreed to not get upset if it didn't work out in their favor. He then went on with the details from the outing and how things seemed to be more complicated afterwards. My head was spinning listening to the story and all of its variables.

Is Sidney gay? Does he like Ashton? Is he straight? Does he like Kendal? Is Emily into Ashton? This is crazy.

"Can I offer a piece of advice, bud?" Owen asked Ashton after both of us took it all in.

"Please, I could certainly use some."

"I think you need to go with your gut and make your intentions known to Sidney. You don't want to be wishing you had," Owen told Ashton. "And you need to find out what this guy wants. Ask the right questions."

Be still, my heart. I love hearing my husband give my brother such sound advice.

"You're right," he responded. "I don't want to have any regrets, and I agree... he needs to know I'm interested, and I need to know if he even likes guys."

"Knowledge is power, buddy. Remember that!" Owen said, clapping Ash on the back. "And then once you have the information you need, can you make sure to give us an update?"

"As if Sophia would ever let me off the hook!" Ashton replied, almost laughing. "Of course, I'll let you *both* know how it plays out."

11

ASHTON

After Sophia, Owen, and Bowie left, I sat down at a picnic table, with Mabel at my feet. I thought about my past and the promise I made to myself about not letting fear and insecurity get in the way of my happiness. I had come a long way since the experience I had with Louis. My sexuality was a special part of me that made me who I was, and I wasn't ashamed of it anymore, and I wasn't hiding it. I knew that accepting who I was made it possible for others to accept me. And that hadn't changed.

Owen's words were repeating in my mind. He was so right. I couldn't be afraid to ask the important questions. I couldn't be afraid to find out the truth, even if the truth meant rejection. I had learned from my mistakes, and I wouldn't allow history to repeat itself. But it was taking the next step that was going to be new territory.

I knew I couldn't ask Sidney at work what his dating preferences were. It wasn't the place. I needed to be professional and respectful at the hospital, some light flirting excluded. Even if we were alone in a break room, talking about it could make him feel awkward or uncomfortable.

He and I needed to hang somewhere together where there would be no chance of other people from work interrupting or just showing up. Asking him to dinner or to a movie seemed premature, since I still had no idea if he thought of me as just a friend from work. It had to be a type of guys outing where we could have deeper conversation and really get to know each other. I supposed the best option would be getting tickets to some kind of event and trying to make it clear that I wanted to get away from all of our coworkers. That way, we'd only have the two tickets, and he wouldn't think to invite others.

Where could we go? I wasn't even sure what sport was his favorite, and all the major stadiums were at least an hour drive away. A festival maybe? That way, there would be a bunch of different things we could do. But where? I guess it was close to Halloween. Yes! I'd get tickets to Shady Brook Farm, and we could explore. They had games, food, drinks, haunted attractions, live entertainment, and more. It was perfect! And if he said he couldn't do it, I'm sure I could get someone from the family to go with me. Okay, I was doing this.

THAT NIGHT, I went in and told my boss at the Tap House I had to put in my two weeks. She was very understanding of my increased workload at the hospital and told me she would get my remaining shifts covered if that was okay with me. And frankly, it was more than okay. I said goodbye to everyone on the shift and vowed to keep in touch as much as possible. That was one very much needed box checked off of my to-do list.

When I got home, I ordered two tickets for the farm's haunted festivities online and then prepped myself to ask Sidney to go out with me. The thought had occurred to me to wait until I saw him at work and casually bring it up, but there was too much uncertainty of when I would run into him there or be put on the same assignment with him, so I decided to muster the courage and send a text.

> Me: Hey! So, I don't think I mentioned how much I love going to festivals. There's one going on over at Shady Brook Farm for the Halloween season, and I have a couple of tickets. Interested?

> Sidney: Are you kidding? I love this time of year! Tell me more.

> Me: The tickets are for any night over the next week, and we can choose. It's the general admission package. I have off Thursday and Saturday. How about you?

> Sidney: I'm off Thursday and Friday. Let's do Thursday then!

> Me: Sounds like a plan! Do you want to meet there at the entrance at 7:00? If you put it into Google Maps, it's easy to find.

> Sidney: Perfect! I'll see you then.

I gave his last text a thumbs up, thinking a heart might not be the right call, and then immediately planned my outfit, making a mental note not to tell anyone about our outing until afterwards.

For as nervous as I was to see where it would lead, I couldn't deny the excitement that was flowing through my veins.

THURSDAY EVENING CAME, and I had to admit my palms were sweaty on the drive over there, and all I could do was wipe them on my jeans and pray they stopped before I met up with Sidney. I kept having to remind myself that if I got rejected, life would go on. What was the worst that could happen? He tells me he's not into men or tells me he's not into me. I could handle that. I needed to calm down.

After arriving at the farm, I scoped out our meeting spot, and since he wasn't there yet, I had time to collect myself and prepare for how I would greet him. A friendly hug seemed like the best option, especially since I didn't know any cool hand shakes. And lots of guys hugged each other. There was nothing weird about that.

"Ashton! Hey!" I heard him call from about twenty feet away.

I lifted my head to take in his presence and had to catch my breath.

"Sidney! How are you?" I went in for the type of hug I'd give one of my brothers. And he accepted, holding it a second longer than Oliver or Elijah would.

"I'm great! Ready to do this?" he asked, eyebrows raised.

"I was born ready. Let's go!"

The pathway to the main attractions was lined with flickering jack-o-lanterns, their grinning faces casting unsettling shadows. A chilling wind rustled through the skeletons hanging from the branches of the trees, and the distant sounds of ghostly wails and creaking doors set the mood.

"How do you feel about haunted mazes?" I asked Sidney, staring at the spooky labyrinth of towering corn hulking in front of us.

"I prefer them to the house variety, where you can't see where you are going most of the time, but out of all the options, haunted hayrides are my favorite."

"We can do the hayride after this!" I smiled and motioned with my hand for him to follow me in.

Within seconds, we were deep into the maze. The further we walked, the more my heart pounded, both from the threats of what could jump out from the darkened corners and from Sidney staying so close beside me as we moved through the narrowing corridors of leafy stalks.

Suddenly, a guy wearing all black started chasing us with a chainsaw, and we ran with fright until we stumbled upon the exit. But it took me a minute to gain back my composure.

"Did you hear how loud I shrieked when that guy came out of nowhere?" Sidney asked with lingering fear in his voice.

"Hear you? No! It must've been drowned out by my screams!" I exclaimed.

We both had a laugh at how two grown men were scared of a costume and fake machinery and proceeded to hop in line for the haunted hayride.

I guess we are gluttons for punishment.

In the growing darkness, lights glimmered from the edge of the cornfields. A dense fog rolled in, curling around our teetering wagon. The distant howls of wind, or perhaps something less natural, drifted through the air, adding to the mounting tension. Suddenly, a figure dressed as a scarecrow crept out from the corn, its ragged clothes and hollow eyes causing a collective gasp from the passengers. As the wagon turned a bend, we entered a dilapidated graveyard scene. Tombstones were crooked and overgrown with creeping vines, and skeletal hands seemed to reach up from the earth.

Further along, the ride plunged into an old abandoned barn that creaked and groaned as if protesting our presence, and the scent of must and decay filled the air.

I shifted uneasily on the bench next to Sidney, who stared out into the chaos solemnly. And ghostly laughs echoed from afar.

I'm ready for this to be over.

Within minutes, we were out of there and headed back down the road where we first got on. Sighs of relief and cries of joy flooded the wagon when it came to a screeching halt.

Thank God!

"You ready for some cider?" Sidney asked when we were free to roam.

"Are you a mind reader? Yes, please!"

Once the two of us had drinks in our hands, I guided Sidney over to an empty table away from the crowd. I figured it would be a good opportunity to dive deep, one I couldn't afford to pass up. We sat down on opposite sides, facing each other. He began making small talk, and I waited for an opening.

"So, I've been wanting to ask you something that's been on my mind for a little while now. It's a bit personal, so feel free to share only if you're comfortable."

He leaned toward me, clearly intrigued. "You have my attention. What's up?"

"Well, we've been spending some time together, and I've really been enjoying it." I took a breath and let it out, keeping my eyes locked with his. "I guess I'm just curious about your dating life and what you're looking for. Are you seeing anyone, or are you interested in dating right now?"

"I'm actually not dating anyone at the moment, but that doesn't mean I wouldn't. Why do you ask?" He took a sip from his drink and then placed his cup down on the table in front of him.

I cleared my throat and continued, "I've just been thinking about our vibe and how well we get along and what our connection might mean. I know this might be forward, but are you open to dating someone from the same sex, or is that not where your preferences are?" As the words were coming out of my mouth, I could barely believe I was saying them. Last year *me* would never.

Sidney paused for a moment, considering his response.

"I appreciate you being upfront about it. I'm honestly open to dating people of any gender. And I have." He smirked and threw me a wink before picking up his cider again. I sipped along with him, trying to process what just happened.

Did he just tell me what I think he did? Did I hear that correctly?

"Wait..." I said after a few gulps. "You've dated both men and women before?" I bit the inside of my mouth to try and stop myself from smiling.

"Yes, I have. Is that a problem?" he asked with slight concern in his voice.

"A problem? No! It's just the opposite actually." I finally pushed aside my overwhelming nerves and allowed a grin to spread across my face. "I have too."

Sidney smiled and raised his cup in the air. "Well, look at that. It seems we have more in common than I thought."

I brought my cup to his and then held my stare as we both sipped the cider. We sat there for a minute, quiet, taking each other in. And then I broke the silence. "I'm very glad I brought it up."

"I am too. Maybe we can just take things slowly and see

where they go?" Sidney asked me, his eyes still locked on mine.

"Yeah... maybe we can." I responded playfully, fully aware he was reading me like a book.

He knows I want this.

12

SOPHIA

Owen was in the studio, and I wasn't expecting anyone. But to my lovely surprise, there he was, glowing with a smile that could probably be seen from the moon.

"I thought I'd stop by and give you an update about last night with Sidney," Ashton said when I opened our front door.

The knocking had Bowie running all over the place. "Well, hello! You're looping me in? To what do I owe the honor?" I inquired with a sarcastic undertone.

"Stop it. You know why I didn't share the other details at first."

"Right, right... I was getting married and all that."

"I just knew the saga of my potential dating life could wait until you and Owen returned from your honeymoon. Are you going to invite me in, or do we have to have this conversation right here?"

"Sorry, come on in. I got caught up in the excitement of your unannounced visit, not that I'm complaining." We made our way to the living room. "So what's up? Where did you go with Sidney last night?"

"I got us tickets to Shady Brook. We had a lot of fun. And something big happened."

"Shady Brook, huh? What, did one of you get scared and pee your pants?" I laughed at my own joke.

"Very funny, but no. Should we get comfy?" Ashton sat down on the couch and was quickly joined by Bowie, who never missed an opportunity to cuddle up. I sat down beside them, ready and excited for whatever it was my little brother was about to lay on me.

Did Ashton go for it? Did they kiss?

"Tell me! What is so big that you wanted to come over here this morning and tell me in person?"

"I know you're on the edge of your seat, so I won't keep you in suspense any longer. It turns out that Sidney... well... he's just like me." Ashton began petting Bowie and couldn't take the smile off his face. "He dates both women and men. It's all about the connection for him."

I took a second before reacting, fully enjoying the moment with him, knowing how this revelation must have made him feel. And then I couldn't hold it in any longer. "That's so great, Ash! Wow! So many thoughts have to be going through your head!"

"I'm still processing all of it, for sure, but I instantly felt incredibly seen as soon as his words were spoken. I mean, I *knew* we had a vibe between us. I could feel it! But even still, I was half expecting him to tell me he was straight and just thought of me as a friend, especially after seeing the way he interacted with Kendal at the bar."

"I totally get your doubts, given the circumstances. And I guess knowing he's open to dating people of either gender doesn't mean he's not interested in Kendal. But it *does* mean he could be interested in you," I responded.

"Exactly! I definitely feel like we have a good connection and that something may happen between us. But I'm trying to manage my expectations. Kendal, or another woman, or honestly, another man for that matter, could be his person. And I still might be getting my hopes up for nothing, but I think I'd rather look at last night as a win." Though the fact that Sidney dating someone else was already on Ashton's radar as a possible outcome, I loved that my brother put himself out there and had a chance with someone he seemed to really like.

"I'm pulling for you, buddy. Kendal is my girl, but I would love to see you get the guy. You deserve it, and this is the first person you have met that you have felt this way about who feels the same way you do about dating. Dare I say it's meant to be?" I was always afraid of jinxing things, but I also loved a good story of fate.

"Thanks, Soph! I'll keep you posted." He gave Bowie one last scratch behind her ears and then stood up from the couch. "I should get going. I have work later and still have to take Mabel for a walk, do some laundry, and get some other chores done."

"I have to get a few things done too before our job tonight at Parx." I walked him out, Bowie following closely behind. "Do you think you'll say something to Kendal about Sidney?" It just occurred to me that she might not want to try and date the guy if she knew Ashton really had a shot or if she knew he was bisexual. One thing I learned from having a brother who dated both men and women was that others struggled to accept their preferences.

"I'm not sure if I should say anything or if I should just let him tell her when he's ready. On one hand, it's his personal business, not that he's ashamed of it or embarrassed by it. But on the other hand, if she found out first, I would want her to tell me. And she is like family. Maybe I should mention it."

"It's admirable that you want to be respectful to him, but I don't think it's a problem for you to give her a heads up. Maybe just give it some thought." We said our goodbyes, and I took Bowie inside.

IT FELT good to be back at the Xcite Center. The last time we were here was for the Candlebox and Bush concert. That was an amazing night, and even though the coordinator, Claire, had said she wanted to use us again in the future, we weren't counting our chickens. Her asking us to do this event made us feel appreciated. It showed she really thought highly of our work and trusted us with another artist. And I couldn't believe I might actually get to have a conversation with Kelsea Ballerini!

Ever since I heard songs from her first album on the radio, I'd loved her. And over the last couple of years, I had also turned Owen into a fan of hers. She was sweet, talented, funny, and beautiful. Her songs got stuck in my head for days, and I had truthfully been wanting to attend one of her shows for a while, so I felt very fortunate to be hired as a photographer for this event.

The protocol was the same as the other concert we did at Parx. We had to be there for the pre-show to get some backstage stage takes of Kelsea with her band and the fans who had bought passes to the Meet and Greet. Owen and I were only there for about fifteen minutes, before it happened. It was brief, but it still happened. Claire gave us an up close introduction to everyone performing. There were two opening acts, who had just gotten their start in Nashville, and then of course, Kelsea Ballerini and her band.

Is this my life now? Where I get to meet and photograph and rub elbows with famous singers? Have I made it? I mean, have we?

We tried our best to play it cool in the moment, which as many people know, is very hard to do unless it's a regular occurrence. And even so, with this particular artist, I think I still would have had some difficulty acting like it was no big deal. But we said hello, smiled, exchanged dialogue about the venue and the incoming crowd, expressed how much we loved her music, and then we received our instructions for the night. After capturing footage backstage, we were to head out to the sides of the pit area to capture action shots from each song, ensuring we had images of her, the band, and the special effects.

Owen went to the right of the pit, and I went to the left. This was one major benefit of hiring a photography duo. And James Taylor was the best business around.

That's what I tell myself when I go to sleep each night anyway.

Kelsea sang every one of my favorites and many more. She even told stories before some of the songs to help the audience understand why she wrote it or the inspiration behind it. I always loved when songwriters would do that! It gave me deeper insight and made me feel like I knew them better. I could have spent several more hours there listening to her sing and watching her dance around, but sadly, it all had to come to an end eventually. Everyone demanded an encore, even though she left us more than satisfied. But the lights came on, and we knew it was truly over.

Until next time, girlfriend! And I pray there will be a next time.

Owen and I met up with Claire once the place had emptied out, and she once again told us that she'd be hiring us for another concert there. Last time she said it, we assumed she was probably being kind and probably said that to all of the photographers she hired, but we believed her now. She even mentioned having a busy lineup in the spring and would be contacting us soon for available dates.

This is our life now. Somebody pinch me.

"We'll get everything over to you within a week," Owen told Claire before we wrapped up to go home.

"Sounds great! You two make such a good team," she said and then wished us a good night.

"I agree, you know," I told Owen once she was gone. "We do make a pretty good team." I moved in to wrap my arms around his torso, locking my fingers behind his back.

"In more ways than one," he replied, kissing my forehead just the way he knows I like it.

13

ASHTON

David Bowie once said, "I don't know where I'm going from here, but I promise it won't be boring." And it was the one quote that had been flashing in my mind ever since I left Sidney at the festival. I didn't know what was yet to come or how things might progress with him. Only time would tell. But I had a feeling things were about to get interesting.

What I did know was how I was starting to feel about him. And I also knew there was a definite vibe between us that was more than just friends. That much was obvious. What I didn't know was how he felt about Kendal or any other potential prospects he might have had. Because, just like me, he said it was about the connection, and he could be into anyone from either gender.

I had to take things day by day and hope for the best. But I still needed to decide if I was going to tell Kendal what I had found out. She and I were very close, and she was even closer with my sister, which made her almost like family. However, Sidney had a right to his privacy and the right to open up about his life to who he wanted, when he wanted. Far be it for me to tell a story that wasn't mine. Maybe if something came up that took the conversation in that direction, I could make the decision right then if I would share what I knew. That was the only fair way for me to move forward with the information. I was secretly hoping she would find out on her own though.

She does always know the scoop on everyone, usually making everyone's business her business in some way or another.

I went to work that night a little apprehensive but elated at the same time.

The schedule, clear as day, indicated that I was not in fact working with Sidney tonight. But that didn't mean I wouldn't run into him. There was always a chance. And the good news was Kendal wasn't working with him either. But just like I had a chance of seeing him, so did she. I would just have to put it out of my mind as best I could, letting the cards fall how they may.

It turned out I was teamed up with Emily for the shift, which meant she also wasn't working with my man. My heart skipped a beat at the possibility of perhaps really getting to call him that one day. Emily was a great nurse too, so though I wasn't exactly happy to not be with Sidney, I wasn't upset either at the pairing.

"Hey, Ash! How lucky are we to be teamed up all night?" Emily said in a bit of a flirtatious voice as she approached me by the NICU. She was cute and funny, but my attention was elsewhere.

"Yeah, lucky us!" I tossed my stethoscope around my neck and snagged a pen to put in my pocket since there were never any around. "We should probably get started," I said, heading toward my first patient's room while my mind was still with Sidney at Shadybrook Farm.

THE NICU WAS SOFTLY LIT, a gentle hum of machinery punctuating the quiet. We moved with practiced efficiency among the cribs, each filled with tiny patients fighting for their strength.

I adjusted the settings on a ventilator, my brow furrowed in concentration. "Looks like Baby Cole's oxygen levels are stabilizing," I said, glancing over at her, while she was gently swaddling a fragile infant named Zoe.

Emily smiled, her voice warm. "That's great news! It's been a tough few days for him." She carefully tucked the blanket around Zoe, who stirred slightly but remained blissfully unaware of her surroundings.

As we finished our tasks, we shared a moment of quiet, standing side by side, watching over the precious bundles of joy. The weight of our responsibility hung in the air, but so did a profound sense of hope. Outside, the world felt distant, but within those walls, each heartbeat and each tiny breath was a victory worth celebrating.

This is why I went into this field. This is why I love my job.

We made our way out and down to the break room for some caffeine. To our surprise, it was already occupied by a few staff members, including two familiar faces.

"Oh, look who it is!" Emily whispered to me as we walked in.

"Crazy seeing them in here together, right?" I asked, thinking maybe she'd have insight on the relationship the two of them have.

"I don't think so. They're friends, and Kendal is totally hot for Sid," Emily responded just before joining them.

Tell me something I don't already know.

I followed her lead and greeted both Kendal and Sidney kindly.

"I guess we all needed a break, huh?" I voiced to the group.

"It's been a wild night here at the hospital, Ash," Kendal replied, smiling and staying close to our object of affection.

"This is the first time I've had a minute to breathe since I began my shift," Sidney said. "How has your night been?" He locked eyes with me and then sipped his coffee.

The vibe is definitely still there.

"It's been eventful. Emily and I were in the NICU for hours." And I couldn't help but notice that Kendal's eyes did not leave Sidney's face, regardless of who was speaking.

She's a smitten kitten. And so am I. This won't end well.

"Listen, I was about to ask you before we were interrupted," Kendal addressed Sidney, rolling her eyes facetiously at Emily and me. She guided him back over to the coffee machine but was still in earshot, and her voice traveled. "Would you want to get breakfast after we clock out? I know a cute little place right down the road."

We had agreed that each of us would go for it, so I couldn't be mad at her. And even if he said yes to going, it was *just* breakfast. Our date was way better and lasted way longer than it would take to eat a meal. But it was still a date, or it was at least an outing that she wasn't inviting the rest of us to. And he was definitely picking up on that.

"Just me and you for breakfast?" he asked Kendal, glancing over at where Emily and I were still standing, mugs in hand, pretending not to listen.

"That's what I was thinking," Kendal confirmed. "I'd like to try to get to know you better. I mean, if that's okay with you." She put her right hand on his left shoulder. I could see it lingering there out of my peripheral.

"I guess that works. I'm sure I'll be famished by then." Sidney accepted the offer, but he didn't seem overjoyed.

Is that for my benefit? Does he really like her but wants to downplay it with me in the room? Or is he just going as friends and coworkers in an effort to not be rude?

"You know, we could go too and spy on them from another table. Want to?" Emily proposed, chuckling softly, noticing I was bothered by what had just transpired. But I knew that wouldn't make me feel any better. In all fairness, I felt like the two of them needed to hang out to see if there was anything there, and I needed to accept that.

Sidney made his way to the break room door, looking back over his shoulder to try and catch my attention. He gave me a nod that I only assumed meant that he'd hoped to see me later. And then he was gone. All I could do was smile, but that quickly faded when Kendal walked over and playfully shoved me.

"Game on, little bro!" she laughed. "My turn!"

"Yeah, I heard. Have fun!" I replied coolly.

She did a little hair flip and then pulled Emily away with her. My heart sank, but I was secretly praying they'd discuss the way he feels about dating while they were together.

AFTER MY SHIFT was over in the morning, I drove home thinking of nothing except for the two of them sharing a meal. Kendal was very attractive, and she was funny and charming. It surprised me that guys weren't regularly lining up to date her. But I also knew she was weird about being in relationships.

I don't know if weird is the right word, but she never

seems like she wants to be in them, even when she really likes a guy. Maybe she truly enjoys the single life and having fun. I can't fault her for that. Being able to do your own thing whenever you want has its advantages. If things don't work out for me soon with someone, I might find myself traveling down that same path.

I decided to go home and get some sleep, cuddled up with Mabel, and then figure out my next move when I woke up. My brain was exhausted from work and worrying about how well breakfast was going.

Maybe I'll text Kendal in a few hours to see how it went. Or maybe I'll text Sidney to ask him out again. Or is it his turn to initiate? Should I even care about whose turn it is when I know someone else is after him too?

When I dozed off, I had a wild dream that involved all three of us. It was so vivid that it felt like real life. I was standing with Sidney at the lake, holding his hand and looking out at the water. All was peaceful within, and I felt like I had finally reached the point of companionship I had desired. Moments passed like clouds floating across the sky, and just when I was about to lean in for a kiss, I sensed a presence among us that threatened to snatch away every drop of happiness I had let myself absorb. When I turned around, Kendal was there, reaching her hand out for Sidney to grab. He succumbed to her advances and pulled himself away from me to join her in a tight embrace. I stared at the two of them with shock splattered all over my face. He began to release her grasp on him, and I felt relief flooding my body.

He doesn't feel anything for her. He's realizing it now.

And just as I took a step toward him, she moved in closer, and she kissed him. He let her. And he kissed her back. And he kept kissing her back. I backed away slowly, in disbelief of what I was watching. I called out his name, once, but he ignored me. They wrapped their arms around each other and continued to kiss, passionately and lustfully, as if I had never been there. I lost him. She won. It was over. And as I walked defeatedly down the path, further and further away from them, I woke up.

What the hell?

I sat up in my bed, my heart racing, my palms sweaty. That was so real. I never dreamt like that in my entire life before. I was invested, and I knew it, and there was nothing I could do about it.

Does dreaming like that mean you are seeing into the future, like a premonition? What if it does? What if it's a warning for things to come?

Pins and needles formed in my chest. I felt so sick I could throw up. The only person I could think of who knew what this felt like and had way too much experience with it was Sophia. She'd know what to do and how to calm me down.

Thank God for her.

14

SOPHIA

"Ashton, what is it? You sound frantic," I said to my brother when I picked up my phone. "Are you okay?"

"I need to talk. I think I'm losing it." His voice was shaky with fear.

"Did something happen? Tell me. I'm here for you."

"I'm not sure if anything actually happened or if it's going to. Maybe I'm just being paranoid. I don't know, Soph. I'm freaking out."

"Take a deep breath, and let it out." I used all of the strategies I'd used on myself over the years to reduce my anxiety. "What exactly has you so worried?"

"Kendal asked Sidney out for breakfast. He accepted, and they went this morning. I tried to take my mind off of it and get some rest, but when I fell asleep, I had a dream that they were very much into each other, even... physically expressing it." Ashton 's voice sounded a little choked up there at the end of the sentence. It was obvious the thought of Sidney and Kendal hooking up was too much for him to bear.

"Let's play the worst case scenario out, okay? What is the worst thing that possibly came from them grabbing breakfast?" I tried to lay it all out for him to gain a healthy perspective.

"I guess they could've gotten to know each other better and realized they get along pretty well. Maybe they hugged and kissed goodbye at the end?"

He was really looking for me to assure him this didn't happen, but I knew how alluring Kendal was and knew all of what he just said could've happened.

"I suppose they may have hit it off. Let that sink in a minute, the potential that Sidney does like her. Sit with it. Breathe it in. He might." I gave him some time to process. "And if he does, it still doesn't mean he isn't interested in you. He could be feeling it out with both of you. He could be feeling it out with more than both of you. Think back to when you were talking with *Kira*, while still having a real interest in Louis."

"Yeah, I guess you're right. He might be trying to see who he has a better connection with and where things go with both of us. I can respect that." He paused briefly and then cleared his throat. "But what if it's her? What if she's the one?"

"Ash, if Kendal is the one, or if another person is, that means you're not. And that's okay. That also means your person is still out there. You are so young. I wasn't with my person when I was your age. It took me a few more years."

"I know, but I know we have something between us. I feel it whenever I'm around him. He and I have to be endgame."

"You and him might be!" I said positively. "And that'd be awesome! But I want you to mentally and emotionally prepare yourself that you guys also might not be."

"I promise to keep my head on straight, but I'm not giving up hope."

"Ash, I would never tell you to, nor would I expect you to."

"I'm going to write in my journal and listen to some music. Those are my two best calming techniques. I appreciate you talking with me."

"I like those for you! And take Mabel for a walk too. Fresh air is always good for boosting your mood and reducing anxiety."

"Will do!" He hung up, seeming slightly more relaxed than when I first answered his call.

I FOUND out that I do not have celiac disease. The results came in from my blood test I had done, and they showed I was negative. That was a relief. However, it also meant that something worse could be going on. Feeling good about ruling something out was very short lived. I still had the colonoscopy looming over me for December, and I was worried how I'd make it through Thanksgiving being unsure about my health. The procedure was still over a month away, and I had to constantly find ways to distract myself from thinking about it.

Fortunately, Owen did an amazing job of helping take my focus off it. He did all he could to keep us involved with the business and plan holiday events with family. Halloween was a couple of days away, and he had already arranged for us to join Elijah and Bethany in taking Hope out to trick-or treat, along with my parents. Ashton had to work this year, but he asked us to take pictures and videos.

Hope decided she wanted to dress up as a black cat this

year, and she played the part very well, purring every five minutes. We met at my parent's house around five o'clock that evening, and then we traveled around the neighborhood for a couple of hours, ensuring Hope's bucket was full. Bowie and Mabel walked with us and were dressed as pumpkins together. It was a successful night of trick-or-treating, followed by some warm apple cider and a hunt through Hope's candy to check for unwrapped items and each of our favorites.

As soon as Halloween came to a close, my mind went straight to wanting to decorate for Christmas. I, of course, like all other years would acknowledge Thanksgiving, at least for that one day, but I needed the joy and spirit of the lights, music, and trees more than ever before. Owen agreed that we would go to any means necessary to cheer me up and continue to take my mind off worrying about what could be wrong with me.

We lined up some work for the months of November and for December, including three weddings, family holiday photo shoots, engagement pictures, an arts festival, and a baptism. All of this would keep me busy enough that I wouldn't dwell on the possible outcomes of my colonoscopy, too much. And by Christmas, I would know what's wrong with me for sure. I was praying it was something minor that could be treated easily or taken care of with a permanent lifestyle change and not something I'd need surgery for or, well, the worst case scenario, need to do chemotherapy. I really didn't want to go there in my head, but I also needed to be realistic. The doctor could find cancerous polyps and could be concerned that more would develop, which would mean even more colonoscopy procedures in my nearer future. But again, it could be nothing very serious at all, and

I knew what Dad would say to me right now. He'd say, "Don't worry until you have to."

I knew that was the right approach. It was the best approach, all things considered. But I couldn't help it. I was scared. I was truly very scared. Nothing anyone said was going to stop me from trying to mentally accept the fact that I could be sick, but I was definitely praying for the best outcome.

"HEY! I HAVE A SURPRISE FOR YOU!" Owen said, coming into the bedroom as I was lying there on the bed with Bowie, his hands hidden behind his back.

"A surprise? For me? What's the occasion?" I knew he was kind and thoughtful, but I couldn't imagine why he would randomly be getting me a surprise at the beginning of November.

"I know it's not a special occasion or anything, and Christmas isn't until next month, but I also know how stressed out you've been over having to get the procedure done, the preparation you have to undergo beforehand, getting put to sleep, the unknown, and all the rest that comes after with waiting for your results. So, I thought I'd come up with something aside from work and family activities to try and distract you from worrying." He sat down on the bed next to me, revealing a large tan gift bag, and urged me to reach inside.

"Owen! You are the sweetest person alive. You didn't have to do this for me." My eyes filled up at the gesture. One tear fell down the right side of my face.

What did I do to deserve him? Was I a saint in another

lifetime? Did I run an animal rescue shelter? How did I end up with such an amazing guy as my husband?

"I know I didn't have to." He wrapped his left arm around my waist. "I wanted to help you. And I know how much you love sunflowers and how much you enjoy a challenge."

"You are absolutely right, on both accounts. One thousand pieces will definitely keep me busy too!" I laughed, staring at the puzzle box in my hands.

"Well, I'm planning on joining in the fun, if that's okay with you."

"I wouldn't have it any other way, baby. Thank you so much!"

He kissed me on the forehead the way he knew I loved it, the way I've loved it since the first time he ever did it. I melted gently into his arms. Somehow, Owen always made me feel like I could handle anything that came my way. He made it seem like big problems weren't so big, and he gave me strength. No one in my life was able to do that in the same way as him.

"Should we get started now?" he said as he stood up from the bed, fixing the disheveled look of his clothes. "I'll go clear off the coffee table."

"Now works for me. No time like the present!" I grinned widely and leapt from the bed, Bowie in tow. "The puzzle pieces are not food, girl." I informed her once we got into the living room.

I'll be so mad if we're missing pieces and find them in her mouth or chewed up somewhere.

She sniffed the box as I put it down on the table. "No! Go get your toy." And within minutes, she had herself occupied with a yellow squeaky ball by our feet.

"Edges first, right?" Owen asked me, pouring out the pieces.

"It's the only way."

And the next few hours were lost completely in focus, laughter, and mastered teamwork.

We'll have this thing done in a week. And then what? I guess we will have to find other methods of taking my mind off things.

15

ASHTON

I had a rare three o'clock in the afternoon to eleven o'clock at night shift upon me. This only occurred a couple of times a month, and I welcomed the variety in my schedule. It meant I could be in bed before midnight, snuggled up with Mabel, unless a better offer came my way, which hadn't up to this point.

I was working with a team I hadn't worked with much before, so it gave me a chance to learn from them and share some of my knowledge as well. We were assigned to the emergency room, and my job was to monitor vital signs and manage ventilators, and I had to be ready in case any patients coded or arrived in critical condition. It was exhilarating to be in this particular area of the hospital because of its fast paced nature and was typically more action packed than the other departments.

I WENT to the locker room on my break to check my phone since we're not allowed to have our devices on us during our shifts, with the exception of our individual pagers. Hospital policy prohibits cell phone usage while working to reduce distractions. I was sure some people may have wanted to keep theirs on them, but I always supported the rule. I never wanted to be responsible for making a mistake, especially something avoidable or careless, when it came to our patients.

What's going on? Why do I have so many texts and missed calls?

I looked at my phone to see that several members of my family had been trying to reach me in the last few hours. And I knew something happened. I knew something very bad must've happened.

I suddenly had a sinking feeling in my stomach. Chills spread through my entire body. I had to read the texts and listen to the voicemails, but I didn't want to.

Are my parents okay? Did something happen to Sophia? Hope? Liam? Was there an accident? Breathe.

I decided I wasn't going to listen to the voicemails and read all the texts right then. I needed to actually talk to someone and get every piece of information available. I called my mom, seeing that she had been the first to try and contact me.

"Ashton!" My mom said, sniffling. I could tell she was crying. "Please get home right away. We have some bad news."

"Mom, what's going on? I didn't read all of the messages. Is someone hurt?"

"We have to fly out to Atlanta. Your father is booking flights as we speak."

"No! Is it Liam?" I asked frantically.

"It's not Liam, honey. It's Bradley. Come home."

"Bradley? What do you mean? What happened to Brad?"

"He's in the hospital, but it doesn't look good. I'll explain more when you get here."

"Okay." I took a deep breath and stood up. "I'll be home soon."

I let my supervisor know there was a family emergency, and she got the rest of my shift covered. I drove back to our house, worrying so much about Brad, about Paityn, and about my seven-year-old nephew.

Both of my parents were upstairs when I walked into the house. I darted up the stairs to find them and announced I was there. Since my room is at the top of the landing, and the door was open, I could see that my suitcase was already on my bed, set to be packed. Dad came down the hall and approached me with a hug. The sadness was visible in his eyes. I could almost feel his pain.

"I need you to pack as quickly as you can. I was able to get flights for all of us. Your mother and I, you, Sophia, and Owen will be flying out at midnight. Elijah, Beth, and Hope will be on an early morning flight tomorrow."

"What about Oliver and Chloe? Are they coming too?" I asked, still trying to process all of this. I didn't even know what *this* actually was.

"They are working on it and should be there sometime tomorrow."

"Dad, what happened? Please, just tell me now. I can handle it."

"Isabel, can you come here?" My dad called for my mom from their bedroom. She was with us in less than a minute.

"Mom, what happened to Brad? Was there an accident?"

"Sit down for a minute." She pushed the suitcase over and sat down on the bed, my dad joining her. I followed and parked myself in my computer desk chair, facing the two of them.

"Okay, what happened to him? Is he not going to make it?" I asked, with panic in every word.

"Your sister found Brad in the foyer of their house earlier. He had just come back from a run." My mom said with tears streaming, her voice choked up.

"She found him? What? Passed out? Was he breathing?"

"He wasn't breathing. He was lying there on the floor. She called the ambulance to come get him. Thankfully, Liam was at aftercare for school, and Paityn hadn't picked him up yet. She was upstairs getting ready to go get him when Brad came home."

"Do they know exactly what happened?" The different possibilities were running through my mind.

"The doctors told Paityn he went into cardiac arrest."

"But did they say he had a heart attack? Because they don't always mean the same thing." I looked back and forth between my mom's face and my dad's face, trying so hard to understand.

"No, but there was a cardiac episode, causing him to fall over and lose consciousness." Mom started to cry into her hands.

"It's not looking good, son," Dad said while consoling Mom. "Let's get packed up and over to the airport. We have a flight to catch."

SOPHIA AND OWEN met us at the airport. Thankfully, our neighbor agreed to watch Mabel and Bowie while we were gone. Once we were all together at our gate, a call was made to Paityn to check on her and Liam and to get an update on Brad. But there was no update. Though he had been initially taken to the emergency room, they transferred him to the ICU.

I knew from working at the hospital that the intensive care unit was where different types of equipment and medicines were used to help support blood pressure, heart rate, and oxygen levels, and it was where they took the sickest of the sick. Even though he was in good hands, there seemed to be no improvement over the time he'd been brought in.

"Hey, Owen went to get some drinks. How are you holding up?" Sophia asked me when we hung up with Paityn. Her eyes were red and puffy, as if she'd been crying for hours. Brad wasn't a sibling by blood, but he had been a part of our family for so long. He was our brother.

"I don't know. I'm still trying to imagine how it all happened and why. I see stuff like this a lot as a respiratory therapist, but I still can't accept that it happened to him. He's young and healthy and had no preexisting conditions. It just doesn't make sense." I looked over at my parents, who were standing together at the window staring out.

"The doctors will figure out why. Let's just pray that he pulls through."

"I will. I am. But... do you think he was pushing himself too hard? I remember Paityn saying he was stressed out with the restaurant for a while, and then he was preparing for these marathons, and he has had his hands full with Liam too. I wonder if it all just caught up with him." Stress was known to cause severe health issues, and I'd seen a lot of related issues even during my short time working at the hospital.

"It's very possible. I suppose it could have been brought on by a variety of things though." She took a deep breath and let it out. "It's probably best not to let our minds run wild. Let's just wait for the doctors to figure it out."

"Well, as you know, that's easier said than done, Soph."

"You're right. You're absolutely right. Listen to me. I've been doing the exact opposite of what I'm telling you to do with this whole situation involving my own health," she admitted.

"I think we can all agree it's hard not to do." I let out a long sigh and then wiped the sweat from my forehead with the back of my hand. "I hope Paityn gets answers soon."

"Hey, it looks like we're starting to board. Let's get in line," Owen said, returning with drinks.

We were in our seats about twenty minutes later with very full bladders. Thankfully, however, the flight to Atlanta wasn't very long, just over two hours, but I knew I wouldn't be able to hold it. I got up to use the restroom as soon as they gave us the green light, and Sophia joined me in line.

Like brother, like sister.

"We will get through this whole ordeal, no matter what," she whispered in my ear as we were waiting for a vacancy.

"I hope you're right. I'm so scared for Liam and Paityn, but I don't want us to lose Brad either." I flashed back to when we had to say goodbye to Harley, the ache almost hitting with renewed force.

Once we were back in our seats, I slid my airpods into my ears and listened to some music by Noah Kahan. He had become one of my favorites over the last few months.

Something about his songs really put me at ease. I closed my eyes and shut everything else out. And five minutes later, we landed. Well, it felt like that anyway.

———

IT WAS ALMOST three o'clock in the morning, but my sister and nephew would be at the hospital, so we went straight there. We found Paityn and Liam in the waiting room down the hall from Brad's room. Approaching them, I could see the distraught in their faces. There hadn't been a revival, and there hadn't been a miracle.

"How is he?" Dad asked, seemingly already knowing the answer but hoping, like we all were, for a different one.

"He's still hooked up to machines, and they're monitoring activity. But there hasn't been any change." Paityn began to sob immediately.

Everyone moved toward her to comfort her together. A giant family hug felt so good right now, even though I knew it wasn't doing nearly enough to keep Paityn together. She asked us to come to Brad's room with her to see him, telling us she already got approval for us to go in before official visiting hours began, and without a word from anyone, we followed closely behind her.

Liam ran in and hopped up in the chair placed beside the bed. He put his hands into a praying motion and looked up to the ceiling. After that, there wasn't a dry eye among us. He had to pull through, for that kid's sake.

"When are Bradley's parents getting here?" Mom asked Paityn, who was now pulling a chair over to the other side of the bed.

"They should be here momentarily," she responded,

wiping tears from her face. "I'll go back out to the waiting room shortly."

"No," I interjected. "I'll go. You stay here. He needs you." I looked at the machines and then at Brad lying there, but not really there, and then I looked at Liam. "They both do."

"Okay, that's fine. Thank you, Ash." Paityn reached over to hold Brad's hand. I could hardly stand there for one more minute.

"I'll go with you," Owen said, ushering me out of the room.

As soon as we made it into the hallway, I let it all out, completely falling apart.

16

SOPHIA

I stayed with my family for about ten more minutes, but then I needed to go for a walk as well. Staring at him like that was too much. My chest was tight. My stomach was knotted. All I could think about was how devastated my sister and my nephew were going to be if Brad didn't make it and how much of a hole he'd leave in our family and his. His parents would lose a son, their only child.

When I reached the waiting room, Brad's parents were just arriving. I greeted them and then made my way to the chapel. Owen followed, while Ashton took Mr. and Mrs. Davis to be with the family.

Thankfully, the chapel was empty when Owen and I entered, so we could have a private conversation after lighting some candles. I had so many thoughts running through my head, thoughts I only felt comfortable sharing with my husband once we were out of earshot of the others.

"Do you think he'll wake up?" I asked him when we sat down in a pew toward the back.

"I think miracles do happen, and I'm not giving up hope here."

"I overheard the nurses talking on my way back to the waiting room. They were at their station, and one of them mentioned organ donation. The other confirmed that Brad was an organ donor. I wanted to yell at them for talking about him that way when he was still alive, but I didn't have it in me."

"Sorry you had to hear that," Owen said, comforting me. "I wouldn't have blamed you if you did, honestly. It's too soon to be having that type of dialogue, especially when his family could be in listening range."

"Right after you and Ash left, Paityn told us more about what happened. They have cameras installed inside the house and outside on the front door because of Liam, so she was able to pull up footage on her phone through the app once she got him to the hospital. Apparently, he was having trouble walking up to the house and was holding his chest, and then he fell to the floor once inside. Paityn found him a couple of minutes later." I caught Owen up with what he missed, and I was counting on him sharing his opinion.

"It's good she found him when she did. He might have a fighting chance now. But something caused him to go into cardiac arrest in the first place." Owen squeezed my hand, knowing I would need it.

Why did this happen?

"Let's keep praying," I insisted. "Maybe Brad has a guardian angel up there somewhere." We sat there a while longer, pleading for everything to be okay, for him to wake up and be out of this nightmare, and for all of us to be out of it too.

THE HOSPITAL ROOM was quiet except for the sound of the machines and the occasional shuffle of nurses' feet outside the door. The fluorescent lights overhead casted a sterile, almost too-bright glow across the room, but it was the faces surrounding the bed that commanded all of the attention.

Bradley was pale and still, lying there. His chest rose and fell with the aid of an oxygen mask, but his eyes were closed, his features drawn in exhaustion. The heart monitor next to him provided a steady rhythm, the soft beep offering a sense of calm that was fragile, as if at any moment his state could shift.

His parents sat on one side of the bed with my sister and Liam on the other. My parents and Ashton went to get food and meet up with Elijah, Bethany, and Hope. Owen and I remained, standing at the end of the bed repeating prayers we said in the chapel. The silence was deafening.

A text from Mom popped up on my phone asking for us to come down to the cafeteria, so we grabbed my nephew to allow him a chance to stretch his legs a bit and to give Paityn some privacy with Brad and Mr. and Mrs. Davis. Once we got to the hospital's dining area, we saw the whole group sitting at a table, Hope holding onto her stuffed elephant that Ash gave her for a birthday gift a couple of years ago. Eli said she slept with it every night and always took it with her when she was scared. I totally understood. I'd carry around a stuffed animal with me too right now if it was more socially acceptable in society.

"Aunt Soph! We made it. Are you okay?" Hope asked me in the sweetest little four-year-old girl voice I had ever heard. Her empathy at such a young age was remarkable.

"Hi, Hope! Come give me a hug!" I held out my arms to

welcome her in. "I needed a big one of these from you," I said while she was wrapped around me.

"I give good hugs too." Hope pulled back from me gently to see my face, her eyes seemingly searching for answers. "Liam, are you okay?" She moved her stare from me to him and began to make her way beside him.

"Daddy is in a bed and won't wake up." His bottom lip quivered. "I just want him to wake up." Hope put her arms around him, and the two of them stayed wrapped up in each other for what seemed like five minutes, though it may have only been fifteen seconds.

"Let's relax down here a minute and try to eat something, okay, bud?" I asked Liam, urging him to sit at the table next to me and Owen. "We can bring something up to Mommy after."

Liam agreed, and we all tried our best to distract both he and Hope from thinking about the figurative elephant in the room. We updated Eli and Beth on Brad's status when the kids were distracted, and we made the best of it with hospital cafeteria food.

THE NEXT FEW hours went by in slow motion. Time stretched in this space, not moving so much as lingering. It was a place suspended between hope and despair. Our family gathered together in one of the waiting areas, taking turns visiting with Brad, tired eyes and anxious hands fidgeting with phones or folded together in laps. The clock on the wall ticked forward, each minute marking the slow erosion of our patience. A few of us sat upright, as if alert for any sound, while the rest slumped in chairs, lost in the quiet chaos of their thoughts.

The light shuffle of nurses and doctors in the corridors was a constant, their white coats and surgical scrubs offering brief, fleeting glimpses of the world beyond the waiting room. The air felt thick, very heavy with uncertainty. The coffee machine, on the far side of the room, seemed to mock the stillness with its occasional gurgle, while the vending machines lined the walls, offering distractions that no one really wanted. A child ran past, his laughter sharp and out of place in the thick tension of the room, while a few seats away, an elderly man pressed a hand to his forehead, eyes squeezed shut, trying to shut out the sound of his own heartbeat.

Sometimes, a nurse would appear at the door, her expression unreadable, and everyone turned toward her at once, a collective intake of breath, only to find out there was still no news. The waiting started to feel like a slow march, a passage of time that refused to reveal any answers. But there was nothing to do but to keep waiting.

It had reached the time where we would be allowed to check in to our hotel, reservations Dad made once we got to Atlanta, and everyone really needed a bit of sleep. Paityn suggested for us to freshen up and get some rest and asked if we could take Liam with us.

"I'll call if there are any updates, but otherwise, can you all plan on coming back early in the morning?"

"Oliver and Chloe should be here in about an hour," Mom told her. "He texted me a few minutes ago. You won't be here alone long."

"Thank you. And I'll be okay until they get here. Brad's parents are going to come back up for a while after they eat."

"Okay, we're going. But call if you need anything. Our

hotel is close by," I said, taking Liam's small hand to guide him out into the hallway.

She closed the door behind us, and even though I couldn't see her, I knew she was crumbling. Maybe it was our sisterly connection, but I could feel it. And I didn't blame her. If I thought I might lose Owen, I too would be inconsolable.

DAD RESERVED four rooms at the nearest hotel with availability, and somehow they were all on the second floor. We checked in, got ourselves settled, and then met at the main restaurant to have some dinner together before calling it a night. Collectively, we agreed it was best to turn in as early as possible, just in case Paityn needed us at an unexpected hour. Hope and Liam were basically dozing off in the booth before we finished our meal. And I felt that. Owen and I had plans for lights out immediately after getting back to the room. None of us could carry a conversation at this point. The only things left to say were how much we wished this never happened and how much we hoped for good news the following day.

As I was falling asleep, there was a tightness in my chest but a slight release of struggle simultaneously. I had spent months worrying about my own health and what *might* be wrong with me. I had played out every terrible scenario in my head, the worst outcomes and how I would deal. And I would be lying if I said I still wasn't scared. I thought so much about what could have caused the issue that sent me to the emergency room that day. And here we were in a nightmare, a true tragedy, facing an ordeal so much worse than all the things I had been having anxiety attacks over.

Suddenly, in the stillness, the panic for myself was slowly unwinding. A realization crashed over me that there were no truths to my stress, only fears. Restless, I rolled on my back, staring up at the ceiling, the fabric of my mind unraveling. My pending so-called doom felt small and distant in comparison to what was actually playing out in real time with Bradley. I could almost feel the weight of my concerns lifting, as if they should have never held such gravity in the first place.

I would get through whatever it was that came my way. I was strong, and I had a support system, an amazing one. I had options, and I had time. Life may had thrown me a curveball, but at least I could process and move forward with one brave foot in front of the other. Brad didn't have those luxuries. He didn't have a warning. All he had was the *possibility* of a recovery, the possibility of a miracle.

I curled my body up next to Owen's and used the comfort of his warmth to gently drift away to dreamland. There, I could escape everything we were currently going through, if only temporarily.

17

ASHTON

The next morning came too quickly for my liking. I spent a good chunk of the night tossing and turning, unable to stop thinking of Brad and whether or not he would make it. The idea of Liam growing up without a father replayed over and over again in my head until I eventually fell into a dream, where it was years in the future. Liam was all grown up and ready to graduate high school, and when we got to the ceremony, everyone was there except for Brad. *Was* it a premonition? Was he not going to survive this? Would there be more cardiac episodes if he did survive?

By the official start to visiting hours, all of us were in the waiting room, even Oliver and Chloe. We hadn't seen them until after we woke up because everyone turned in so early the night before. But for the first time since the horrible incident, the entire family, along with Brad's parents, was together and eager to find out if any progress had been made.

"Hey, you're all back," Paityn said, pure exhaustion in her voice.

"Honey, did you sleep at all?" Mom asked her, approaching with a side hug. "Do you want to get some rest? We'll stay here."

"I slept some. I'll be okay. I really don't want to leave him." She bent down to a squatting position and waved Liam over to join her. He raced over without hesitation and leapt into her arms.

"Mommy, is Daddy awake yet?" Liam inquired softly.

"He's not, buddy. I'm so sorry." Paityn stared at his face, really wanting to tell him something that would make him feel better, but what could she say? And from the vibe I was getting, it didn't seem like she'd ever be able to.

Mr. and Mrs. Davis stood up and went to go be with their son. My nephew sobbed against my sister's chest. The rest of us glanced from one person to another, searching for something uplifting to say.

"Why don't we take turns going down to the chapel to light candles and say prayers?" I suggested, lifting Hope from my lap, where she'd been sitting from the moment we got settled.

"That would be nice, Ash," Paityn said, standing up with a smile that she was clearly forcing.

We decided to go in groups, and I was in the first group with Eli, Beth, and Hope. Next in the rotation were my parents with Paityn and Liam, and then Sophia and Owen went down with Oli and Chloe. Each group stayed there about twenty minutes or so and then returned, giving everyone time to say what they needed to. But it still just wasn't enough.

Once we were all back together, I volunteered to walk with Paityn back to the room to check on Brad, curious for an update myself. But when we got close, his parents were in the hallway, holding onto each other.

"What... what's going on?" I asked aloud to no one in particular.

"The doctor asked us to step outside," Mr. Davis said, all choked up.

"Wait, did something happen while we were gone?" Paityn asked. Her eyes were wild and her voice frantic.

"A nurse was inside checking on him, when his monitors started beeping loudly. She paged his doctor and asked us to leave. The doctor arrived just before the two of you." Mrs. Davis began to sob.

Paityn tried to comfort them, her eyes filling up from the fear of it all. I watched, wanting to do something and feeling helpless. And just when I was about to turn and head back to the rest of my family, it happened.

The door to his room opened, and the doctor appeared, his face lined with concern. He looked at Paityn and then at Brad's parents. They stood there frozen. He took a deep breath and then cleared his throat before speaking.

"I am so sorry to have to tell you this, but we've done everything we could. Bradley's condition worsened. He was having another cardiac episode, and we couldn't bring him back. His heart was just too weak."

"Do you mean... he's gone? He's just gone?" Paityn cried out. "No, I don't believe it. He can't be gone!" She pushed past the doctor and into the room.

I texted the family group chat to tell them to get down to Brad's room. I added a 911 so they'd hurry. Then I followed behind Paityn to see for myself because I couldn't believe it either. Mr. and Mrs. Davis stayed behind to ask the doctor more questions, but I knew it'd only be a matter of time before they were in the room trying to make sense of it all.

My sister sat on the left side of the bed with her hands

stretched out across his body, begging for him to wake up. I stood next to her, thinking my presence would provide her with comfort, knowing deep down that nothing could.

Mom, Dad, Soph, anyone... please get in here. I'm not good at this kind of thing. I don't know what to say.

"How can he be gone?" Paityn cried, not looking up at me.

"I don't know. I can't understand it either," I told her, staring at his pale and lifeless face.

Why didn't our prayers work?

Just then, his parents and my parents appeared with a nurse. I excused myself and left Paityn to be with all of them in private. I was so thankful for the reprieve. Another minute in there, and I'd have lost it completely and not been able to pull myself together.

When I came out of Brad's room, Sophia and Owen were approaching, and I could tell from their faces that they already knew. Thank God, because I couldn't speak. Tears began flooding from my eyes.

"Ash, let's get you out of here," Owen said. And the three of us walked back to the waiting room, where the rest of the family sat in silence, even my niece and nephew.

Does everyone know? Did they tell Liam and Hope?

I was unsure of what to say, and I was still having a hard time processing, so I kept quiet. We all did. The ticking of the clock on the wall was the only thing stopping me from falling into a daydream, where I could pretend none of this was real. I glanced around at everyone, wondering what was going through their minds. Liam was lying on Oliver's lap from the chair beside him, practically asleep. Hope was already out cold, cuddled up with Bethany. The rest of us sat there, waiting, wanting this to not be true.

But it is. And we have to accept that. And we somehow have to help Paityn and Liam accept that.

THE FUNERAL WAS HELD on a gray, overcast afternoon, the clouds hanging low like a blanket over the small cemetery in Quakertown, Pennsylvania, Bradley's hometown. A slight breeze rustled the leaves of the old oak trees that lined the perimeter, as if the earth itself were whispering a delicate goodbye. The air smelled faintly of damp soil and freshly cut grass.

A small crowd had gathered around the grave, our faces solemn and eyes either fixed on the casket or turned inward with private grief. Some of us were dressed in black, others in muted colors, but we all wore expressions of quiet sorrow. A few people stood apart, avoiding eye contact with the others, perhaps not knowing what to say or how to grieve in such public moments.

The casket, made of polished wood with brass handles, gleamed under the dull light. It rested at the edge of the grave, surrounded by white roses and chrysanthemums, their soft petals barely moving in the wind. A single red rose lay atop the casket, placed there by Paityn's trembling hand.

At the front, the priest stood with his head bowed, his voice low and measured as he read prayers of remembrance. The words seemed to hang in the air, heavy and full of meaning, but also distant, as though the space between the living and the dead was growing with each passing syllable.

Mrs. Davis dabbed at her eyes with a handkerchief, her shoulders shaking slightly. She was flanked by Mr. Davis, who stood stiffly, his hands clasped in front of him, his face expressionless but tight with emotion. The sounds of the ceremony were punctuated by the occasional sob or cough and the scrape of shovels as the workers prepared to fill the grave.

After a few moments of silence, the priest gestured for the pallbearers to step forward, which included myself, Elijah, Oliver, my dad, Owen, and a cousin of Bradley's. Slowly and carefully, we lifted the casket and began the somber procession to the grave. We lowered it into the earth with deliberate, reverent movements. Each lowering seemed to take with it not just the body, but a part of everyone's hearts as well.

As the first shovelful of dirt hit its hard wooden top, Paityn cried out, a raw, anguished sound that seemed to ripple through the cemetery. Her grief was palpable, and for a minute there, the formality of the ceremony broke down into pure human emotion. Others wept quietly, not yet ready to let him go.

The atmosphere felt thick with the weight of memory and loss, as if time itself had paused to honor him. Finally, the crowd began to disperse, some walking slowly back to their cars, others giving their final goodbyes to Bradley's parents and my sister. The grave, now completely filled, stood as a silent testament to a life once lived.

18

———

SOPHIA

Thanksgiving week was upon us. Paityn decided to stay in Buckingham for the holiday instead of going back to Atlanta. My sister was able to get the manager of her restaurant to take care of things in her absence, and Liam's school was notified of Bradley's passing, so his time away was excused.

This year, given the circumstances, Owen and I were having dinner with my family for Thanksgiving instead of going to eat with Owen's family as we had in the most recent years. Everyone was still so fragile and really needing the support of each other. My mom even reached out to Mr. and Mrs. Davis to invite them to join, but they declined, saying they were taking some time to themselves to process and grieve. And we all understood that people deal with loss in different ways.

With it being this close to the end of November, it also meant I only had a couple of more weeks until my dreaded colonoscopy appointment. But I felt better about it now. There was something about losing someone you love, especially so suddenly, that just shifted your perspective. I knew

I'd most likely be overtaken with anxiety on the morning of the procedure, but for now, there was a new calm inside me when I thought about what the doctor might find or how I would handle whatever it was that came next. If Paityn and Liam were strong enough, so was I.

"Are Eli and Beth coming over at all on Thursday?" I asked Ashton when he stopped over after work to have breakfast with Owen and me.

"No, I think they're taking Hope over to Bethany's parents this year, but they should be coming by the day after for leftovers," Ashton replied, allowing Bowie to slobber all over his face. "Who's still your favorite?" he said between kisses. "I know, I know, I am. Look, your mommy's getting jealous."

"I'm not jealous. Lie to yourself if you have to, but she will always be *my* baby," I laughed and called Bowie over to my lap. "So, how are you holding up?"

"I guess I'm doing alright. It's only been about a week since the funeral, but I've been trying to make peace with it a little more each day." He took a seat on the couch next to me. "Actually, going through all of this has really shown me that we're not promised tomorrow. And it's made me think about how I shouldn't wait so much for things to happen."

"That's great, Ash. I completely agree. Life is short, so no point in not really going for what you want."

"Yeah, so... I invited Sidney to Thanksgiving dinner." He ran his right hand through his hair, attempting to not seem too pleased with himself. "And he accepted."

"What's this I hear?" Owen asked, walking in from the bedroom. "You have a date for the holiday? That's my guy!" Owen nudged him playfully, the two of them laughing, while I was stunned with pride in my little brother.

"I'm so happy for you!" I said as I stood from the table

and signaled with a tilt of my head for them to follow me to the kitchen. "This is awesome. I finally get to meet this mystery guy!"

"You just might not want to add Kendal to the guest list. I'm pretty sure he's interested in me and not her, but you can never be too confident, and I mean, it's hard enough that we all work together."

"You don't have to worry about that. She'll be with her family." I turned on the stove to make some eggs, while Owen brewed a dark roast, its aroma floating through the air. "Rae and I are supposed to see her Saturday though, so maybe I'll hear where she's at with him or with anyone else she's potentially talking to."

"I'll expect you to FaceTime with me the minute you get home from being out with them." Ashton smirked and sipped his coffee from the mug Owen handed him.

"Well, let's not get crazy," I responded with a chuckle. "I'll give you a summary of my findings as it pertains to you."

"Good enough!" Ashton said with a nod of contentment.

I finished making the eggs and distributed them to their plates. We talked a little about how we felt the mood would be at Thanksgiving dinner the following night and what we could try to do to boost the energy. It was going to be hard, for a while, but that didn't mean we couldn't still make an effort to make the most of things.

SINCE MY PARENTS loved to cook, and my sister did it for a living, I was able to sit this one out and spend my time occupying my nephew and the pets in the family room.

Owen and Ashton helped, along with our special guest, who I had to say was very charismatic and quite suitable for my little brother.

"So, how is it we are blessed with your presence this Thanksgiving?" I asked Sidney.

I swallowed hard, unsure of the answer myself and suddenly nervous that I'd brought up a sore subject, like both of his parents had passed away or something equally tragic.

"I'm an only child, and my parents decided to take a cruise this year for Thanksgiving, so it was either I worked or ate by myself. None of my friends from over the years live nearby."

"How nice for your parents. Where did you live before moving to Doylestown?" Owen asked.

"I grew up in Maryland, about twenty minutes from Baltimore. I always wanted to live in a small town though, so when I saw the posting for the nursing job at the hospital, I jumped at the opportunity," Sidney shared with us.

"City life isn't for everyone. That's for sure," Ashton interjected. "I learned that when I was living in Nashville my first two years of college."

"So you discovered there's no place like home then, did you?" Sidney smiled at my brother with what looked like tiny stars in his eyes.

This guy was taken with my brother. There was no doubt about it.

"Absolutely!" Ashton replied. "Does anyone want a glass of wine?"

"I can't drink wine, Uncle Ash! I'm only seven," Liam answered playfully.

"Okay, buddy, good point! Guess that leaves more for

the rest of us," Ashton joked back and then went to retrieve a bottle and some glasses.

While he was gone, I took the opening as a way to find out the scoop on what's been going on with Kendal. I figured I might not get another one before the night was over.

"I hear you know my good friend, Kendal, from the hospital too. Dark hair, dark eyes, a respiratory therapist like my brother." I began to pet Bowie, who was lying at my feet, in an effort to seem nonchalant.

"Ah, yes, Kendal. She and I have become friends. I like her."

I wasn't positive how to take his last comment.

Does he like her because she's fun to be around? Or does he like her in a romantic way? Just because he's here at our house for the holiday doesn't mean he has ruled out any potential with Kendal, or anyone else for that matter. He and Ashton are still in the early stages of getting to know each other.

"She's great! I've known her for many years. Have you hung out with her a lot?"

Give me something to work with!

"Not really, honestly. A few of us had drinks one night in town. Ashton was there too actually." He glanced back toward the kitchen at my brother, who was still selecting the wine. "And Kendal and I had breakfast together once. But other than that, I just see her at the hospital. We text sometimes though."

Hmmm... they text? I wonder what they talk about. I will definitely have to bring it up when I see her on Saturday. I need to know!

"That's cool. Well, where is my brother with the wine?" I changed the subject before he got back so it wouldn't be awkward. When I heard the bells on Mabel's collar jingling, I knew he was seconds away. That dog was his shadow.

"I chose a bottle of merlot. I hope that's okay with everyone," Ashton said, setting the wine and glasses down on the table, along with the opener.

"Works for me!" I picked up the merlot, uncorked it expertly, and began pouring. "Ash, I remember the one year Mom tried to put jingle bells on Harley's collar around this time, and she wasn't having it."

"Oh yeah, Harley hated the bells! I forgot all about that." My brother took a sip and then scanned the space for where Mabel had made herself comfortable. "I don't know why, but this girl loves them. I think she'll be mad when we take them off in January." He chuckled and then inched ever so subtly closer to Sidney on the couch. I had to respect his efforts.

Sidney sipped his wine and pretended not to notice, letting a slight smile spread across his face as he put his glass down in front of them. These two were obviously very into each other. Anyone could see that.

"Liam, I hear you are really good at spelling. Can you spell a few of your favorite words for me?" Sidney asked my nephew in the cutest way, making sure he felt included. And I was starting to really see why my brother and my friend were both catching feelings for the guy.

"I can spell!" Liam exclaimed. "I can spell *turkey*, and I can spell *potato* and *picnic* and *cookies*—"

I stopped him before he got too carried away. "Why don't we try those words for now? Spell *turkey* for us." And he did. He spelled it slowly and perfectly, and then he pronounced it again at the end, just like any good spelling bee contestant would do.

"Great job, Liam! Spell *potato* next," Sidney encouraged him.

And he did. He repeated the pronunciation and then moved onto the word *cookie*. He spelled that perfectly too. He was a master. And we let it go that he forgot about *picnic*, collectively feeling pretty confident that he would spell that word correctly too.

"You really are amazing. It's clear you've been practicing," Owen praised him. "I think you deserve a *cookie* since you did such a great job spelling it. What do you think?"

"Yes, please!" Liam's face lit up. "Now?" He stood up from the floor, where he was playing with a couple of toy dinosaurs.

"Now is as good a time as any. Let's go!" Owen rose from his chair next to me and held out his hand for Liam to take. My nephew really needed all of this right now. It was going to be a long road ahead until he felt *normal* again. They walked to the kitchen, and I followed behind, giving the lovebirds some privacy.

WITHIN THE HOUR, my parents and Paityn had prepared everything on the menu, and my dad was starting to carve the turkey. I knew my sister needed to be cooking in an effort to take her mind off the absence of her husband. She had always been that way, using work as a distraction. And from the sounds of her soft hums, it seemed to at least be temporarily doing the trick. I bellowed for Ashton and Sidney to come to the kitchen, hoping I hadn't interrupted a special moment between them.

They joined us with an empty bottle, seemingly ready

for a new one. Coincidentally, I had just opened another of the same kind, so I took it upon myself to refill their glasses.

"What time are we doing FaceTime with the rest of the family?" Dad asked after he was done slicing thick cuts of turkey breast off the delectable bird.

"Oli said six o'clock *our time* worked for them," I responded.

"Sounds good! Someone please send a text to Eli to confirm they will be available at that time too," Dad asked. And I was on it. I knew they were enjoying time with Beth's family, but hopefully, they'd still be able to join the video call.

Once that was settled, we all sat down for dinner at the dining room table, which was dressed in a harvest-colored cloth and a centerpiece of autumn leaves surrounding a tall flickering candle that smelled like apple crisp.

Mom led us off with grace, and we made a toast in remembrance of Bradley before we began eating. As I sipped, I locked eyes with Paityn, who I knew would need so much more than a moment of silence. There was no doubt she would continue to struggle with Bradley's passing. Liam would as well. But I was going to figure out a way to help them. I just wasn't sure what that was yet.

"Sidney, thank you for considering us special enough to spend your holiday with this year. We have been enjoying getting to know you," Mom said halfway through our meal.

"Thank you for having me. I really appreciate all of you including me and for inviting me into your home. Mr. and Mrs. James, I can see where Ashton gets his kind heart from." Sidney looked at my little brother, and I could feel the spark between them. As a matter of fact, I think everyone else in the room could too.

"It meant a lot that you could be here with us," Ashton spoke up.

"I wouldn't want to be anywhere else right now," Sidney said, his eyes never leaving Ashton's.

"Is it okay for me to give Doug a piece of turkey?" Liam asked randomly, which offered a humorous break in the conversation.

"Honey, no! Rabbits can't eat turkey. They have a strict diet. We've talked about this," Paityn replied sternly.

"I'm sorry, Mommy. He looks hungry. What can I give him?"

"I'm sure grandma and grandpa have some lettuce in the refrigerator or some carrots. We will feed him when dinner is over," Paityn picked up her glass to take a large gulp, now looking more exhausted than I'd ever remembered seeing her.

Girl, you drink all you need to. We got you.

I excused myself to go get some more wine, thinking I could *kill two birds with one stone and* sneak over to gather some lettuce at the same time. For Liam's sake, I made a show of slipping a few leafy handfuls into Doug's cage on my way back to the table and gave my sister a nod.

"Thank you," she mouthed to me before turning to Liam, "See, bud? Doug's all set," Paityn reassured him.

"Yay! He won't be jealous anymore of our food!" Liam laughed and took a forkful from his plate to munch happily right alongside his bunny.

19

ASHTON

Author Joyce Meyer once said, "Patience is not the ability to wait but to keep a good attitude while waiting." And though I've thought about these words over the years, they never seemed more applicable to my life than they were now. I was simultaneously trying to grieve the loss of a loved one while trying to catapult a romance. I didn't know how long either of those things would take, but I was steadily hopeful I was going to be okay in the end. Thanksgiving dinner last night with the family reinforced that even more.

Sidney hung out at the house until after eight o'clock. He even took part in the family call, where I was able to introduce him to everyone. And he handled that like a champ too. And I expected no less.

What I wasn't expecting was how strongly my feelings came on for him before the night was over. I knew I liked him, and I knew how great he was, but I didn't realize I would fall for him so heavily before I even had the chance to kiss him and see what was there. And I *did* want to kiss him. But the timing had to be right.

I wanted to do it as I was saying goodbye. We walked outside to his car, where I thanked him again for being part of things and for being so amazing with my family. The air was fresh, and the world felt distant. I could feel it, the magnetic pull between us. Everything about the evening seemed to push us closer.

But just when I thought it was going to happen, his cell started ringing. His parents were calling from their vacation to wish him a happy holiday. So I let him go and sent a text about a half an hour later to make sure he got back to his apartment safely. He confirmed all was good and told me he looked forward to seeing me again soon.

I fell asleep peacefully, thinking only of him and the potential relationship we could have. I wanted it. I really wanted it. And it seemed he wanted it too. I just had to have faith that things were going to continue progressing.

That's what I had on my mind as I drifted off, which led me to another dream with the two of us at the lake. Except this time, Kendal wasn't there. It was just me and Sidney, and we were in kayaks on the water. It wasn't November at all. Instead, it was a summer day, and we were wearing nothing but our bathing suit shorts. He was paddling along-side me and then halted when we were far enough away from everyone else out there. I stopped paddling too, wanting to remain close to him. And just when I did, he reached out to hold my kayak in place. I looked over at him, admiring how his eyes sparkled in the bright sun, smiling just enough to let him know I was truly appreciating the moment.

When it seemed like he was going to lean in to kiss me, I woke up. Of course, I woke up. Dreams always left you wanting more, at least, the ones that weren't total nightmares. It was like when you dreamt of sitting down to eat an extraordinary meal or dessert, and right when you were about to take your first bite, your alarm clock went off.

Why? Why can't I just have the ice cream sundae?

In the morning, I vowed to not leave anything up to chance with this guy, to not expect things to just happen because it *might* be meant to be. I really needed to put effort into finding out if he wanted to date me. I was all in, regardless of how anyone else felt about him. And if he chose me, they would have to deal with it and move on.

I sent him a text to say hello and included the selfie that he and I took once we were alone in the family room before dinner. It wasn't the best photo of me, but it was cute because we were in it together. Within a few minutes, he put a heart on the picture and replied back.

> Sidney: Those are two handsome fellas in that photo!

> Me: Haha... Right?! Quite the good-looking pair!

> Sidney: Are you going to post that on your Facebook or Instagram page?

> Me: I was thinking about it. Do you want me to?

> Sidney: It seems like something everyone we know should see.

> Me: Okay! I'll put it up now and tag you.

> Sidney: Make sure the caption says something about you spending the holiday with your new favorite person!

> Me: You must be reading my mind.

> Sidney: Great minds think alike. I'll be on the lookout for it. See you at work tonight?

> Me: Yup! I'll be there just before 7:00. Hopefully, we get teamed up!

> Sidney: I'll say a prayer. Later!

Our prayers were answered when I found out later he and I were working together on our shift. There must have been an angel at play, helping dish out an extra helping of luck. Maybe Harley? Or Bradley? It was comforting to think that it was perhaps either of their doing. It was rare to get put on the same assignment with him, so I was grateful, regardless of who or what made it happen.

I went to my locker to hang my coat, and on the way out, I spotted Kendal. She softly punched me in the shoulder, as she usually did, but this time it was accompanied by a strange look.

"I saw your post earlier, little brother," she said, calling me out.

"Yeah? That was from last night. I invited him to have dinner with us."

"That was nice of you. Pretty cozy pic there!"

"I guess so," I responded, trying not to rub it in. "We get along well."

"I can see that," she commented, rolling her eyes just slightly. "Everyone else can too now, thanks to your post on Instagram."

"Kendal, it was a holiday moment we wanted to share. It's not like we are hard launching our relationship."

I wish.

"It's okay, really. I get it. He's super easy to get along with." She strutted by me to get to her own locker. "I'm just giving you a hard time."

"So, you've had more opportunities to get to know him better?" I asked, reminding myself silently that Sophia was planning on bringing it up with her the following night when the girls went out.

"We worked a shift together while your family was in Atlanta." She turned around, her face growing serious. "I'm sorry about your brother-in-law. That's so heartbreaking."

"Thank you. We're hanging in there." My eyes filled up unexpectedly.

Kendal walked toward me. She placed her hand on my shoulder. "Listen, I'm here for you and Soph no matter what. I'm here for the whole James family, regardless of you and me trying to land the same guy, okay?"

"I know. I appreciate that." I pulled her in for a hug. "I think you should accept defeat though," I whispered.

"Ha! I'll know when I've lost. But I'm not out yet," she spoke with confidence that wasn't quite believable, as if she was trying to convince herself.

"I think we will both find out soon enough," I told her, backing up and heading out. "Besides, I'm sure you have some other options if this doesn't work out the way you want it to."

She smiled, assuring me I was right, and with that, I left to go find Sidney.

IT WAS the kind of night that made the hospital feel both alive and eerily quiet all at once. It was busy, but in a controlled, rhythmic way. Sidney, with his calm presence and gentle smile, was prepping medication in the small nurses' station. I was quiet as I observed him, noting how attentive and vigilant he was on duty, even after hours of administering care. He looked exhausted, but in an endearing way, his shirt slightly wrinkled, his hair tousled from the long shift, and his eyes shadowed with fatigue. It was the kind of handsome that wasn't about perfection, but presence. And it was impossible to look away from.

During our break, he suggested we go to the cafeteria and get coffee and snacks. In the elevator, we stood next to each other among the others inside but didn't say a word. And although we weren't alone, I could feel a sense of longing between us. I briefly imagined a scenario where we were the only two people in the lift and Sidney hit the emergency stop so that we would be stuck in it together indefinitely. In my daydream, as soon as we came to a halt, he pushed me up against the back wall and began passionately kissing me, running his hands through my hair and breathing hard with urgency. He paused to tell me how much he wanted me and nobody else, stared deep into my eyes, and then began kissing me again, more aggressively than the first time. And I kissed him back every second of the way.

As if saying no is ever an option in this particular situation with this particular guy.

The elevator jerked to a stop on the ground floor and the doors opened to allow everyone in front of us out. Sidney locked eyes with me, and for a second, it seemed like he just had been imagining the same thing I was. I grinned, stepping out first. Maybe we were so connected we didn't even need to use words to express our thoughts to each other.

"Let's grab our drinks and then take that corner table over there, yeah?" Sidney asked, pointing to the secluded spot.

"Sounds good. I'm getting the largest coffee they have." I stifled a yawn and shuffled toward the counter.

The cafeteria always had the best chocolate muffins, so we picked up two of them to go with our coffee and sat down at the table.

"Ash, thanks again for including me last night. I would've been home alone, probably eating takeout or one of those frozen dinners."

"You don't have to keep thanking me. I wanted you there, and my family loved having you with us. They had nothing but positive things to say about you after you left too."

"That's really sweet. You have a great family. It's obvious how close all of you are to each other, especially you and Sophia," he replied, bringing his cup to his mouth immediately after.

"Sophia and I are tight for sure. She's really been there for me, but we all try to be there for each other." I broke off a piece of my muffin, unable to wait a minute longer before tasting it.

"You're lucky. I never had that growing up, being an only child, so it's very nice to see." Sidney smiled and then dove into his own muffin.

"You're welcome to hang with us anytime you want," I told him, implying I wanted him around. "We do a lot of festive activities for Christmas."

"I love that you invite me to things. It makes me feel like I have a real friend in this town who enjoys my company."

I cleared my throat. "I do enjoy your company, but I don't know that I see you as a friend," I said, blurting it out quickly so I couldn't overthink it.

He picked up his cup again, took a big gulp, and then sat it down, never taking his eyes off my face, while mine didn't leave his. "Do you maybe see me as more than a friend?"

"Um... well, yeah," I responded. "I think after spending the past few weeks together, I would define us as more than friends, if I'm being real with you."

I had promised myself after losing Bradley so suddenly, I would embrace more risks. Life was short, and we only got to do this once, so dammit all, I was taking the leap.

"Good." He popped another piece of his muffin into his mouth, allowing some time for his comment to sink in. "I was hoping you'd say that. I think we are too. And I was also thinking... maybe you'd like to go out again the next time we both have a free night?"

He just asked me out.

"That would be great. What're you thinking?" I tried so hard to play it cool, but I was actually freaking out, my insides sparking like a fourth of July fireworks display. Every time we hung out, aside from that first night we met up in town, it was because *I* had invited *him*. But this time, he was inviting me out.

So. This. Is. How. It. Feels.

"I was thinking about something with lots of lights and festive music. I'm sure you've done almost every Christmas event in the area over the years, but maybe we could find one you haven't been to." He glanced at the face of his phone, let out a sigh, and stood up. "Looks like break's over. Time flies when you're having fun, right?"

We gathered our trash and disposed of it, hustling toward the exit. I then checked my watch almost in disbelief that fifteen minutes had flown by so quickly.

"I haven't done *everything*, and I'd be interested in trying something new with you," I said as we walked toward the elevator.

"Sounds perfect. Let's discuss some more after we look at our schedules and find out when we have off together next."

For the rest of the shift, all I could think about was my upcoming date with Sidney and the fact that he asked me out this time, not the other way around.

20

SOPHIA

I was getting ready to go out with Raelyn and Kendal, but it was always so hard leaving Bowie when Owen wouldn't be home to keep her company. He had decided that since I was going out, he would go down to his dad's boat for the day and go striper fishing. Kevin joined him. Bowie would just have to spend a few hours in her crate snuggled up with her blanket and her favorite toys. We still used the crate when we left the apartment. Otherwise, she would get anxious or frustrated and get into things she shouldn't.

I took her outside for a quick lap around the block and then gave her a treat before saying goodbye. Of course, she gave me those sad puppy dog eyes, telling me in her own way that she didn't want me to go. Unfortunately, we were going to a restaurant that didn't allow dogs to come inside, so she would have to stay home and wait to hear all about it when I got back.

"Don't worry, Bowie. Mommy will be back in a little bit," I said when I reached the front door. "I'm not going far, and I'll give you all the details later."

She wagged and then whimpered, but ultimately, I believed she understood and would be just fine.

I met Raelyn and Kendal at the Water Wheel Tavern, less than ten minutes of a drive away. It was so nice having such a large variety of reputable places to eat in the area. They beat me there, most likely due to how long it took for me to make my departure from my little fluffers.

We were seated at a very cozy table by their large stone fireplace, which was the best spot in the whole restaurant, in my opinion. It crackled with a soft, golden glow, casting dancing shadows across the walls. The room smelled of garlic and roasted herbs, with the faint aroma of seafood dishes and pasta covered in marinara filling the air.

Within an hour, the table was cluttered with empty glasses, half-finished plates of food, and the occasional gleam of silverware catching the firelight. Laughter from our stories permeated the room, and the server brought over the second bottle of wine we ordered just in time. Kendal was about to give us the details on her relationship with Sidney.

"So, we text here and there and have hung out a couple of times," Kendal said, pouring the riesling into all of our glasses. "And one of those times, Ashton and another nurse from the hospital were with us."

"Do you think there's something between you guys?" Rae asked her, picking up her glass to sip. "Isn't Ashton like super into this guy?" As my best friend and Owen's sister, Raelyn was always looped in.

"Yes, but they have an agreement not to let their interest in him affect their relationship," I interjected, sipping my own wine.

"I did make an agreement with Ash, but honestly, from what I can see, Sidney actually might have a real thing for him. It was fun at first to see who might have a chance with Sidney, but it's pretty clear they have a connection."

"Well, what does that mean for you and him?" Rae asked.

"I'm not going down without a fight!" Kendal replied.

"You can't really be serious, can you?" I locked eyes with her earnestly, my disapproval as thick as syrup.

"Soph!" she gasped. "No! Of course, I'm joking!" Kendal sat her glass down on the table and took a beat. "Listen, I like the guy, but I've been keeping my options open anyway, just like I always do. And I can tell Ashton cares for Sidney. I'm out."

"I'm so happy to hear you say that!" I exclaimed. "My brother is developing feelings for Sidney, and I think they have a real shot."

"Yeah... that really is great news. Ashton deserves to find love." Raelyn held up her partially filled glass for us to cling.

"To Ashton!" We all said in unison and then drank to that.

We spent the remainder of our time there going deep about our real issues. Raelyn shared how things were going at the magazine and how Kevin had asked her if she would like to start trying for a baby soon. Of course, we were excited for her, but Rae clarified she wasn't sure if she was ready for that, which led Kendal to mention how she met a woman at the hospital who had recently adopted a child and how it had her considering looking into that process one day. I could actually see Kendal doing that. And I looped the girls in on the prospect of Owen and I getting out of the apartment and buying a house of our own.

"I fully support you and my brother moving into a

bigger place," Rae said. "Your business has been growing, and Bowie could use some space to run around."

"We would definitely want a yard or some type of outside area for her to play in. And what if Owen and I give her a sister or brother?"

"Are you two planning to have a kid soon? You just got married!" Kendal's voice rose to a high pitch.

"What? No, we're not planning that. I meant another puppy!"

"You scared me, girl. Enjoy married life for a little while before you jump into the next stage." Kendal sipped from her glass she'd just refilled. "I'm with you on the new home thing though. You'll have to keep us posted."

We paid our bill and made our way out to the parking lot, where I reminded the girls to send me good vibes for my upcoming doctor's appointment. In one way, it seemed like it had crept up on me, but in another, it seemed I was worrying about it forever.

But I can handle it. I'm strong. And I have another angel watching over me now. Right, Bradley?

THE EVENING before the procedure was finally here. My thoughts were about as organized as a bunch of toddlers trying to line up and make their way outside for recess at daycare. I mostly felt like everything was going to be okay as far as the procedure went, and I also knew I had the right amount of support to get me through whatever came next. But I still had this uneasy pit in my stomach that left me shaky and unsettled.

I had to drink a very revolting solution combined of Gatorade and Miralax. The taste was like nothing I'd ever experienced. I might as well have been on that show Fear Factor, where they have to consume whale snot and boiled buffalo testicles. It was absolutely disgusting, choking down each gulp with tears in my eyes. I barely finished. Several breaks were needed between the chugging, which nearly made me vomit.

When I finally finished, I took myself back to my sunflower puzzle that Owen had gifted me as a way to keep my mind off of worrying. And it definitely worked. That was, until I had to run to the bathroom. I'd known it would be coming, but I didn't quite understand the urgency of it. My stomach rumbled and growled as if staging a mutiny, and I groaned, bent in half, as I awkwardly waddled to the closest toilet. Much to my displeasure and discomfort, I spent the next two hours bouncing back and forth between the living room and the bathroom.

This is no fun at all.

When my stomach settled, I returned to the couch, focusing only on fitting pieces together in different sections of the landscape, and not once did I panic about going into the hospital the next day. Mental notes were made for the future if I ever had to distract myself or someone else from dealing with the anxiety of a main event.

A thousand piece jigsaw puzzle will do the trick!

"Need some help?" Owen asked, pulling me out of the zone briefly.

"Of course! Sit!" I scooted over on the couch for him to join me on my right. His presence alone always made me feel better.

"My dad tells me the preparation for it is the hardest part. He says the night before is the worst, and then you get to have one of the greatest naps of your life after they put you under." Owen made an attempt to calm my nerves.

"My parents told me that as well," I said while completing a flower in the top left corner. "I believe them and you, don't get me wrong. I just want all of this over with. I still have to drink more of that solution in the morning and then get the needle to go to sleep."

"You're doing great, Soph. By this time tomorrow, we will have all of it in the rearview. And whatever the doctor finds, we will face that together."

"Thanks for the *we*. Knowing you'll be with me every step of the way makes me feel like I can handle anything." I rested my head onto his shoulder beside me, my heart swelling with true gratitude.

"You *can* handle anything. You're strong and resilient. But I'll always be here for you, no matter what." He added another piece to the puzzle, a big chunk of the stem I had been working on. "Let's work on this for another hour maybe and then head to bed. Sound good?"

"That sounds perfect. Maybe it will exhaust my brain enough that I'll fall asleep quickly."

"I'll rub your back until you do." Owen kissed my forehead and then pulled me in for a squeeze. "It's you and me, baby."

I smiled for what seemed like the first time all day.

I love him. So much.

WHEN I WOKE UP, the reality of the next several hours set in instantly. I clung to Bowie and Owen for comfort, feeling the muscles in my chest beginning to tighten.

Just five more minutes in bed with them, and then I'll get up and face the day.

I drank the second dose of the prescribed solution, and I

was rapidly sent straight to the bathroom again. Taking one deep breath after another until I felt strong enough to take a shower, I stepped into the tub, my skin tingling from the contrast of the cool air in the room and the heat of the water. I closed my eyes, letting the droplets wash away the tension of the past few days. It felt refreshing and reviving.

Owen took Bowie for a walk while I got ready to go to the hospital. This gave me some time to mentally prepare myself, which included reminders of what our family had recently endured, the amount of support I had, and how I just needed to take everything one step at a time. A lot of people went through things like this, and much worse. I could do this. And I was going to.

Just relax, Sophia.

Once home, we put Bowie in the crate and left for the appointment. The parking lot was packed, so Owen dropped me at the door and went to find a spot while I checked in. When I reached the receptionist desk, I was asked an in-depth round of questions about the preparation to ensure I'd followed the directions properly.

"Did you drink *both* doses, one last night and one this morning?" the receptionist asked me.

"Yes, I did. It was terrible, but I did it."

She seemed unfazed and continued typing. "Have you been on a liquid diet since the start of yesterday?"

"Yes, I have. I'm actually starving and cannot wait to eat later," I said with a soft smile, trying to help myself look ahead to brighter times.

"Good. Have you had any water in the last couple of hours?" she asked me, staring ahead at the computer screen in front of her instead of at me.

"I had a little bit, maybe just under two hours ago. Is that a problem?" My chest tightened again.

"Will you excuse me for a minute while I speak to one of our nurses?"

"Why? Is there something wrong? Was I not supposed to have any water?" I was now freaking out. If they made me reschedule this because I drank less than six ounces of water almost two hours ago to prevent dehydration, I was going to cry right here in front of everyone in the waiting room.

God, please don't let that happen.

When she stepped away, Owen appeared behind me. And I really needed him. I immediately turned around and wrapped my arms around him. He hugged me back so tightly, somehow sensing my distress.

"What's going on? Is everything alright?" he asked me, still locked in our embrace.

I pulled away, releasing tears from my eyes. "I think there might be an issue with me having that bit of water a couple of hours ago. I don't think I was allowed to do that," I explained.

Please don't reschedule me.

"You barely had any, and you needed to have some after going to the bathroom so much. Let's wait to see what the doctor says. Are they speaking to him now?" Owen looked past me over the counter.

"The receptionist said she was going to talk with a nurse."

"Okay, I spoke with the nurse who will be assisting in your procedure." I drew my attention to the woman behind the desk as she filled me in. "By the time we get you ready to see the doctor, three hours should have passed since you drank the water, so you will be fine. Sorry if I scared you. We just need to make sure there isn't any possibility of aspiration while you're under the anesthesia."

I sighed the heaviest sigh of my life. "Thank you! That's such a relief." I latched hands with Owen, and we made our way to our chairs to sit until I was called back.

"You got this. Just breathe, and I'll be here waiting for you as soon as you're out." His voice had a way of soothing me like nobody else's.

AFTER ABOUT TWENTY MINUTES, I was taken back to a small room where I was asked to change into a hospital gown and put all of my belongings into a plastic bag that would be returned to me upon being discharged. Next, the nurse instructed me to lie down and get comfortable in the bed. I spoke to her for a little while about what to expect during the procedure, and as we were finishing our conversation, an anesthesiologist came in to prepare me. He explained what was going to happen, how long I would be out, and what things would look like afterward. The nurse attached the IV to my right arm, and before I knew it, I was being pulled into the room with the gastroenterologist, Dr. Yang. There were two nurses in there with him, along with the anesthesiologist I had met prior. I was asked to go to my happy place in my mind so that they could begin.

Immediately, I imagined being at the lake with Owen. Unfortunately, I only held the vision in my mind for about five seconds before I was out cold. The next thing I knew, I was waking up in a different space across from the room I had just been in with the doctor, and I was all out of sorts. A new nurse was standing next to me, seemingly waiting for me to open my eyes. She offered me juice and a cookie. There was no way I was declining any offered morsel of food right now. It was Friday, and I hadn't eaten a thing since Wednesday!

Owen was brought in to see me a few minutes later, and he stayed with me until I was released. While he was sitting at the right of my bed, Dr. Yang came over and discussed his findings.

"Sophia, I have some good news for you. I did not find any pre-cancerous polyps while performing the colonoscopy. Sometimes, I will find clusters of them, but you had none," he explained.

"That's great to hear. I was honestly expecting it to be worse." I reached for a hand from Owen and continued listening.

"I was also able to confirm that you do not have Crohn's disease, and you don't have ulcerative colitis, which I suspected might be the issue."

"Well, if I don't have either of those, what is actually the problem?" I felt relieved and still slightly concerned simultaneously.

"It seems your colon is very susceptible to high inflammation. You're really going to have to continue modifying your diet moving forward. You'll still need to steer clear of dairy, as well as anything that is high in fat or high in fiber. And remember to limit your caffeine. I'll give you another copy of the list I printed when we first met, the document that specifies what to omit from your diet and what you should stick to or add in. This is going to be a lifestyle change now. Excuse me for just a minute while I grab it for you."

"I don't have cancer. I don't have anything I was scared of, Owen."

Thank God!

"If changing your diet is all you have to worry about, I think that's a win. I'm so happy it's not more serious."

Dr. Yang came back with the list and assured me I was safe to eat a full meal as soon as I left the hospital. He warned me I might have to use the bathroom more the rest of the day, but by the following day, my system should be back to normal. Finally, he informed me I wouldn't need another colonoscopy for five years.

Nice! I'll take that!

"Let's get you something good to eat, shall we?" Owen suggested, standing up. "I'll go to the waiting room while you get dressed, and then we are getting anything your heart desires!"

"Deal! Thank you!"

I got myself out of the bed, pulled the curtain for privacy, and got changed. Thankfully, my bag of belongings had been brought to me while I was waking up from the anesthesia. I strapped on my crossbody purse and swiftly walked out to find my guy. I retrieved my paperwork from the front desk and hopped in the car Owen had already pulled around, with a delicious hot meal being the only thing on my mind.

21

ASHTON

Sidney and I compared schedules and realized the next time both of us had off from work was this Friday night. How perfect! Not that I had a typical weekend like most people, being a medical professional, but I still loved going out on those nights because the environment was good and the vibe was fun.

Like he had suggested, I put some heavy consideration into a Christmastime activity I hadn't already experienced in our area, which was difficult since I grew up in Buckingham and spent so much of my time in the neighboring towns. I really wanted to go to the village with him, where I had so many amazing memories, and it was still on my mind as somewhere to take him before the season was over, but this time had to be new for both of us.

I remembered Sophia had told me about a vineyard nearby that had live music every Friday and Saturday night, along with food trucks. She said the place was huge and had tons of lights everywhere, including on all of the vines. I looked it up and made the suggestion to Sidney. Without hesitation, he was in.

He even picked me up to take me there. This was an actual real date. And what was even better was that Kendal had messaged me during the week to tell me that she was bowing out. Sophia already tipped me off the day after she went out with her and Rae, but it was nice to hear from Kendal that she no longer had interest in trying to date Sidney. According to her, there was just a friendship between the two of them, and she saw way more than that happening between me and him. I respected the hell out of that. And it was perfect timing to get the information before my first date with him.

When we pulled into the parking lot, it was abundantly clear we had made the right decision. The entire winery was covered in bright white lights, going all through the vines and beyond. One of the barns there, called The Chicken Coop, had an archway upon entering that was illuminated by red and green blinking bulbs and featured two small Christmas trees that had been sprayed with fake snow to give off the wintertime ambiance.

The other barn was enormous and had a deck attached at the top of a tall ramp, which included multiple tables with fire pits placed in the center and was decorated similar to the smaller barn, only with more faux snow covered pine trees. However, given the December evening temperatures, not a soul was in sight.

We could see from outside there was a live band of three members setting up about ten feet from the entryway. Sidney opened the door and signaled for me to walk in front of him, displaying the type of chivalry I didn't know I needed.

"After you, kind sir," he said in jest. I did as I was told and then paused for him to reach my side.

"You know, I would've liked to watch you walk ahead,

but I dig the effort." I gave him a quick once over from head to toe. "I hope to get an opportunity later."

"Oh, I'm sure you will. I'm bound to have to use the bathroom at some point." He smiled and began slowly taking steps toward the bar. "That is, if we don't go together," he followed up, turning his back to make sure I heard him.

I'm happy taking your lead tonight!

The winery itself was cozy and rustic but with a touch of modern elegance. The low lights from lanterns cast a warm glow over the wooden beams and polished floors. I looked around to take in the charming and festive atmosphere, finding it hard to believe that I was out with my dream guy at a place where time seemed like it could stand still.

A bartender approached us with a sheet of wines to try and explained how the tastings worked. She distributed two glasses and asked us to choose from the list. We were able to pick six from any of the red, white, and fruity selections. I made a deal with Sidney that he could pick three, and I would pick three.

"I'd like to go with the holiday red, the chilled apple, and the estate white," he told our server.

Great choices!

"I'll have to go with the estate cab, the strawberry moscato, and the dry red blend." I handed the sheet back, lightly brushing Sidney's arm with mine.

He stood to the left of me, looking at my eyes while the bottles were being lined up along the bar. I held his glance, wishing I could freeze the moment. The guitarist of the band struck its first chord just as our wine was being poured. We sipped and rated and sipped the next until we had tried all of our choices and decided on the estate cabernet.

"If we get through this bottle too fast, I'll get us each a glass of our second choice," I offered after he bought the cabernet. We both agreed the apple was our second favorite, but I enjoyed the dry red blend as well. Sophia and Raelyn had definitely turned me into a lover of the reds. I hadn't really had one I didn't like. And Sidney didn't prefer the whites either.

"That sounds like a plan," he responded as we found a spot to sit at a table a few away from the band. "I could see us being here for a while."

"I love the way this place feels," I said, scooting my chair closer to his.

"I love how you feel," he replied, placing his right hand on my left knee. I locked eyes with him again, having another moment I wished I could capture and keep forever.

Where's Sophia with her camera when I need her?

The band played a few more songs as the crowd sang along. We even joined in at one point. The energy was contagious. And so was Sidney's smile. My face was beginning to hurt from the nonstop grinning, but I didn't mind. I hadn't laughed or smiled that much in a long time.

I am really happy. He makes me really happy.

"Thank you for recommending this place, Ash. It's just what I wanted, and needed honestly." He poured the remainder of our bottle into both of our glasses equally.

"I had a feeling we'd like it here. My sister told me some great stories of nights out here with the girls."

"Sophia hangs out with Kendal a lot, right, and her husband's sister?"

"Yeah... the three of them are super tight. You'll have to meet Raelyn sometime. She's sweet like Owen, and so much fun." I sipped the last of my wine, already gearing up for some of our second choice.

I flagged down the bartender to ask for a round of waters, making sure to hydrate a bit before heading home.

"I'd love to meet her. We should definitely make that happen." He gulped down the last drop of his wine, placing his glass back down on the table and brushing his hair back with his other hand.

"Are you ready to try the chilled apple next?" I asked, sliding my chair out and standing up.

"You read my mind." He slid back his chair and stood up. "Let's do it!"

THE BAND FINISHED THEIR SET, and the barn began to empty out. We lingered there as long as we could before it became too obvious we didn't want to end the night. I wasn't sure how discreet I was being, although at that point, I wasn't sure I cared.

Sidney eventually started to clean up the table and make his way to the bar to return our glasses. I followed behind to say goodbye to our bartender, and then we slowly trotted out to the deck. And by slowly, I mean I was confident a sloth could have beaten us out there.

Our date was ending, and I knew I'd see him again soon, at least at the hospital, if not before then. But I suddenly felt incredibly bummed. It took everything in me not to ask him to stay out later with me. I didn't want him to think I wasn't satisfied with our time together or that I was desperate for his attention. So I walked with him all the way to the car, taking in the cold air and Christmas lights that had been hung on every inch of the property. I really did love this time of year. Even though it was edging into winter, I was so happy, and this type of atmosphere made things feel, well, kind of romantic.

"I had the best time with you tonight," Sidney said as we were strolling by the lit up vines. "This vibe is perfect."

"I did too, with you. I'm sad it's almost over," I said without abandon. It wasn't like I was hiding my feelings well anyway.

"Before we leave, I have to ask you something." He paused and faced me.

"A question? Sure, go ahead." I could see from the intensity on his face that this was serious. And I was beyond intrigued.

"Well, I was wondering if it might be okay if..." he dodged my stare as he scanned the vineyard, perhaps a little nervous, and then brought his focus back to my eyes. "Can I kiss you?"

It's happening. He wants to kiss me. He's asking to kiss me. I'm finally going to know what it's like to kiss Sidney. This will tell me if we really have the fire I think we do. This is it right here.

I kept my eyes locked with his in silence until he brought his face closer. "Yes," I whispered to him when his mouth was just centimeters from mine. "I want you to."

With those words, his lips were on mine, his arms around my body, and my hands were in his hair. The passion between us was electric, and the heat was undeniable.

The fire is definitely there.

We kissed for what seemed like an eternity but in reality was only a few minutes. I wanted more. And I could tell he did too. But it was enough for tonight. It was just the right amount for our first kiss.

First of many, I hope.

Sidney eventually drove me home, sporadically touching my left leg and looking over at me from the driver's seat the entire way home. Music was playing, but I couldn't tell you a single song that played. I was in a daze of delight I had never really felt before. And I loved it.

"We should spend some time together again soon," he said when we pulled up in front of my house. "Like, really soon."

"I'd love that." I leaned over and gave him a soft peck on the lips before reaching over to open my passenger side door. "I'll clear my schedule," I teased with a wink.

He smiled and said goodbye, and I watched as he drove away down my street. The date had concluded, and he was gone, but I still had butterflies.

This feels good.

When I laid down to go to sleep, I still saw his face. I saw the look he had right as he asked if he could kiss me and the look he had after he did. I saw the look he had when he left me. And I saw all of it until I drifted away, praying I'd dream about him too.

22

SOPHIA

On our most recent family Zoom call, Paityn shared some important, life-changing news with the rest of us. I know, what could be more life-changing than her losing her husband and us losing a member of our family?

"I've decided I can't live in Atlanta anymore," Paityn stated. "I can't work at the restaurant that Bradley and I invested in together, and I can't live in the house we built a life together in without him there."

"I completely understand," I told her. "I couldn't imagine being in your shoes. It makes sense not to stay."

She explained that one of their silent partners, who also had shares in other local businesses, offered to buy her out and search for new ownership so that all her current employees could still keep their jobs. Paityn had already contacted a realtor to list her house and packed everything she could over the course of a week. The rest of their belongings would go into a storage unit while logistics were being sorted out. She hired a moving truck and then made a plan for Liam to exit school two weeks before the holiday break.

"My plan is to move back to PA so we can be with our family. And I feel like Bradley's parents will cope better with the loss of their son if they can see Liam more."

"Your father and I fully support your decision!" Mom said. "It'll be so nice to have you and Liam and that adorable bunny here with us instead of all the way out in Georgia."

In a few days, I'd be helping them get settled in at my parents' house. With me having been gone a while, they had turned my bedroom into a second guest room, but they also had the option of staying in the basement, which is where they always set up camp during their visits. I supposed they could split up too and let Liam and Doug share a space and give Paityn some privacy. Either way, I was going to have more of my family around me, and I was going to be able to help my sister and nephew try and get back to a better head-space. Although, I knew they would never truly get over this.

"Well, Chloe and I will be coming to join all of you for the holidays!" Oli exclaimed. "We'll be there for a whole week, as long as it's cool that we stay at the house. There will still be room, right?"

"You know we will make it work, son," Dad assured him.

"Thank you so much, Mr. James!" Chloe said graciously.

"I told you to call me Dad, Chloe. Mr. James sounds way too formal," he replied with a smile.

"Just call him Daniel. He likes it when I do," I chimed in with a chuckle.

Truth be told, I don't think he likes it at all that I started to call him Daniel when I was nearing the end of high school.

But it seemed mature, and after I tried it out, it just kind of stuck.

"Yes, Sophia... I love when you address me by my first name as much as your mother loves it when you address her by hers." Dad rolled his eyes, while everyone else laughed.

"Mom enjoys it, and she knows it. Isn't that right, Isabel?"

I'm a comedian.

Ashton changed the subject by expressing to everyone that he had a really nice date with Sidney at my favorite vineyard. I already knew that because he and I tell each other almost everything, but I was thrilled for him all over again. Owen and I both had a way better feeling about this guy than we had about Louis (aka *Kira*), and even the girl he dated for a bit not too long ago. Sidney had good energy, and I could see for myself how into Ashton he was.

Elijah and Bethany updated the family on Hope's academic development in preschool and how she had expressed an interest in wanting to take dance lessons. I could just picture her in a little pink tutu twirling around on a stage and maintaining poses. Then the inquiries started pouring in about the photography business. Some might get bothered about always having to answer questions about work, but I actually loved talking about our jobs and new clients. This time, I had a cool story for everyone, since a piece we had shot was going to be hanging inside the art gallery downtown. That had always been a goal for me, even before I joined forces with Owen, so it was surreal knowing it had finally happened.

"You know, with having a photo featured at the gallery and more concerts lined up with Claire, I'd say we've reached a level of success that might help take us to our next step," Owen said when the video call was over.

I was grateful for more opportunities to work the shows at Parx, and the gallery piece was definitely going to give our business a boost, but I wasn't quite sure what Owen was getting at here.

What next step?

"Things are going very well for us with James Taylor, yes," I agreed. "But what type of step are you referring to? Do you have bigger dreams for us that you haven't shared?"

"I'm always dreaming, baby." He moved in closer from his spot next to me on the couch. "And I think we can make this particular dream a reality."

"Oh yeah? Are you talking about the business or married life?"

"What if I'm talking about both?" A soft grin spread across his face. "Hear me out." He had my attention.

"I'm listening..."

I can tell this is something he feels passionate about.

"I've been thinking that now might be the perfect time for us to do an upgrade," he said without specification.

It has to do with the business and our marriage, so I feel like the possibilities here are limited. However, I don't want to guess too big if he's got a smaller idea in his head about what the next step is.

There was a short pause in the conversation, and then I finally asked him to stop keeping me in suspense. The anticipation was killing me.

"Owen, tell me! What kind of upgrade are you talking about?"

"Okay, I'll put you out of your misery," he conceded. "I think it's time we move into a bigger place, one that has room for a bigger photography studio as well."

"Really? You're ready?" I've been wanting to do this for

the better part of the last year, but I was trying to be sensible and not live beyond our means.

"Don't you feel like we are both ready, Soph?" He grabbed both of my hands and held them tightly.

"Yes!" I exclaimed with so much joy in my heart. "We are ready!" Bowie leapt up onto the couch, sensing the upbeat tone of my voice, and began licking both of our faces in celebration. It was almost as if she understood every word and was just as excited to find out she would be moving to a place with a lot more space.

"We should start looking then," he suggested after getting our girl settled. "I would like to find something with a nice outdoor area for some of our work."

"Of course! I concur!" I replied very excitedly. "That's a must!"

"Great! I'll see what I can find within our budget and current location. We have built a solid client base here, and our families are both nearby, so it makes the most sense to find something close."

"Absolutely! I wouldn't want it any other way," I responded, hugging to seal the deal. "I'll look too!"

JUST DAYS LATER, Paityn had arrived with Liam and Doug in tow, along with a moving truck attached on a trailer that needed to be unloaded. Luckily, with a family as large and as involved as ours, Paityn had a lot of help. Owen had come over with me to my parents' house, and my dad, mom, and Ashton were all there ready to do some heavy lifting. After we set my nephew up at the kitchen table with some crayons and coloring pages, we got to work.

It took roughly four hours to get everything out of the

truck and situated in their designated spots. And once every box and piece of furniture that traveled with them was out, Dad and Owen returned the U-Haul truck back to a local rental store. At least, that part was low stress. My sister still had to deal with getting the rest of her furniture transported to Pennsylvania from Georgia eventually. And she was going to have to handle all of the paperwork for the house once that sold too.

With Oliver and Chloe coming soon to stay for a week, Mom thought it best for my sister and Liam to put all of their things in the basement until after the holidays. Anything that didn't fit in there was stored in the garage or the attic temporarily. That way, my older brother and his wife could sleep in my old bedroom for the week instead of being crammed into the loft, which was really meant for short-term sleeping arrangements.

"I really appreciate everyone lending a hand," Paityn said once we sat down in the kitchen, sweaty and exhausted, at the table with Liam. "It means so much to me to have your support."

"Honey, we're always here for you. I hope you know that," Mom told her while pouring some iced tea into glasses for all of us.

"I can watch Liam on occasion too when I'm not working, you know, if you just need a break or need some time to yourself to figure out next moves," Ashton offered.

"That goes for me too. I love spending time with my favorite nephew." I gave the little guy a wink.

"I'm your only nephew, Aunt Soph!" He laughed and made his best effort at trying to wink back.

I love this kid. He's come so far since the days of calling me Aunt So. Although, it was adorable when he did.

"Thanks, again! I feel very fortunate to have such a

loving family." Paityn's eyes filled up as she picked up her glass to take a sip.

"Well, you know your father and I can babysit too, and don't forget, I'll be retiring soon," Mom reminded us. And we were all so happy for her! She worked thirty-five years as a special education teacher in public schools and did it with such a kind and positive outlook, going above and beyond for her students whenever she could.

"You guys better believe I'll be taking you up on it, especially once I get myself on my feet and start working." She held her stare at Liam and then spoke again. "Actually, Ash, do you have work tonight?"

"No, I have the night off because I work the next two night shifts. I have some tentative plans but nothing confirmed. Why? What's up?"

"I was thinking, if you wouldn't mind..." She moved her eyes from my mom's face to mine. "After everything that has happened, the long drive, and the unpacking of the truck, I feel like maybe a nap and then some drinks out with my favorite ladies might be just what I need. No offense to you, Dad, or Owen."

I gave my mom the nod of approval and Ashton the prayer hand gesture, signaling that I too would love a night out with Paityn and Mom.

"I wouldn't mind at all. I'd love to spend some time with my nephew." Ashton gave me a nod that alluded to me having to owe him one later. "You ladies have fun!"

"Sophia, I'm sorry. That was presumptuous. Mom, you too. I didn't even check to see if you guys had anything going on. I just figured that both of you would be free."

"Lucky for you, I am free," I reassured her. "Owen and I had a quick consultation this morning, but we have nothing else scheduled for today or tonight. I'm sure he won't mind flying solo tonight with Bowie." I retrieved my phone from my bag on the table. "I'll text him to let him know the plan so I'm not springing it on him at the last minute, but I'm sure he'll be fine."

"And I'm free too!" Mom told all of us with enthusiasm. "I haven't had a ladies night in a while!"

I WAITED for Owen and my dad to get back from returning the U-haul, and then he and I went home to take care of Bowie. We had a bite while she was eating, which was followed by a loop around town. Our walks would be much faster if Bowie didn't stop every two minutes for various reasons, but there's nothing to be done about it. The simple fact was she got overstimulated by her surroundings.

Paityn texted me to let me know they were going to come pick me up, since the place we were going was a few minutes drive from our apartment, so I bid farewell to my loves, put on my scarf, tucked my phone in my small black clutch bag, and headed outside to wait for them.

This will be good for my sister. She's been going through so much.

We were at the restaurant Vela only a few minutes later, ready to be seated. I took a peek at the cocktail menu while the hostess found us a table, and a couple of Christmas-themed drinks caught my eye. One was called Naughty or Nice, and the other was a Pear Tree Martini. Both looked and sounded delightful.

Decisions, decisions.

By the time we were settled in at our table, I already knew what I wanted. I figured I'd try the martini, and if it wasn't amazing, I'd do the other next, if there was a next drink, which I was sure there would be. Paityn and my mom also decided to go with martinis, but they chose different flavors than mine.

"We're so fancy!" Mom said when our drinks arrived. And Vela was kind of up there with upscale restaurants in our area.

"When in Rome, right?" I joked, holding my glass up to cling to theirs.

"Thanks for doing this with me tonight. Things haven't been easy lately for me or for Liam." Paityn's eyes filled up as she placed her glass down. God, I couldn't imagine what it was like to lose your partner or to be strong for your kid who had just lost their dad.

"Listen, you don't have to put on a brave face. We all know this is extremely difficult. If you weren't struggling, everyone would be concerned," I told my sister, reaching for her hand across the table from me.

"It all just happened so quickly. I didn't see any of it coming." She picked up a napkin and blotted her face. "Two months ago, he was here. Liam had his father. I had my husband." Paityn took a breath to try and gain control of her emotions. "Now, I'm selling my house, and I've given up my business."

"Honey, things are going to be hard for a while. But I think you made the right decision moving back here with your family. Let us help you get through this," Mom encouraged her.

"I know all of you are here for me. I am so fortunate to have the support that I do from this family. But it's hard. I don't think I'll ever be the same again, and I don't think Liam will be either."

"Let's take it one step at a time," I advised her. "As time

goes on, life will get a little bit easier. You just have to keep putting one foot in front of the other."

"My first step is getting Liam enrolled in school. I'll head over to the district office and see how soon we can get him started."

"Once things are situated with him at school, we will do our best to help you enjoy the holidays. You can worry about work in the new year. And I'm sure the house in Atlanta will sell soon." I tried to help my sister look at things in a more positive light.

"Everything will be sorted out. Just try to relax as much as possible and get some sleep at night," Mom told her. "You don't want to make yourself sick."

Paityn nodded, and we all sipped our drinks, commenting on how lovely the restaurant was decorated and how nice the ambiance was. Everything always looked so beautiful at Christmastime. It made you forget about the cold and the darkness that was approaching in the upcoming months, if only for a little while.

23

ASHTON

My tentative plans I mentioned earlier were with Sidney. He had to work the day shift at the hospital, and I had told him if he wasn't exhausted by the end of it, that maybe we could go over to the village. The way it was lit with over a million lights was definitely a sight to see and something I wanted to share with him. With Liam at the house though, I was sure I'd have to reschedule those plans for another night.

I texted Sidney to give him the update, and to my surprise, he asked if we could take Liam with us. I ran it by Paityn, who immediately agreed to allow me to take him there, saying how it would be great for my nephew. I got his carseat and put it in the back of my car, and we left just after my sister and mom went to pick up Sophia. How awesome was this guy, still wanting to hang out even if a seven- year-old was tagging along? I noticed how I liked him a little more each day.

The first thing we did when we got to the village was check out the gingerbread house displays. It was really hard to pick our favorites, with so many being both creative and detailed, but Liam chose one that had a Nightmare Before Christmas theme. He had discovered a love for Jack and Sally over the last year, so his whole face lit up when he saw it. After spending way too much time there, we took him to get some hot chocolate, with extra marshmallows, of course. I wanted to have his photo taken with Santa, but I didn't feel it would be right without his mom there, so I promised him we'd all come back together.

In exchange for a visit with the big guy dressed in red, we walked back and forth through the tunnel of lights more times than I could count. Sidney was being such a good sport about it too. He had never been there, so every minute was an exciting moment, and I tried to hype it up each time by taking pictures and videos of the three of us, snapping a couple of just me and him to potentially frame at a later date. In all honesty, even if my nephew hadn't been there, I would've had us walking through the tunnel more than once.

"Uncle Ash, will you buy me a present?" Liam asked when we walked into the wizard shop. I had wanted to go in there because I remembered Sidney mentioned liking fantasy and Harry Potter, so I was hoping to get an idea of what to get him for Christmas. But Liam was just as enthused to be in there, if not more.

"Maybe, buddy! Let's see how good you are here," I responded, looking around at all the store had to offer. I was pretty sure Paityn hadn't done much holiday shopping yet, but I still had a concern of overstepping. I took out my phone to capture photos of whatever he asked for so I could quickly text my sister and get her approval.

"I'll be good! I promise!" Liam assured me with a sweet smile.

"I'll be good too, Ash. Promise," Sidney said with a devilish grin.

"I'll have my eye on both of you," I replied playfully.

"I like it when your eyes are on me," he quipped back.

Why am I sweating all of a sudden?

We made a left turn at the corner to walk down the back aisle of the shop. And out of nowhere, a werewolf appeared from a wall with a creepy howl and red eyes. Liam screamed. But so did I. Sidney laughed at our reaction.

Why would someone have put that there? It was the Christmas season!

My nephew, now spooked, took a few minutes to bounce back from the fright, which was only soothed when he saw a large wand at the end of that same aisle. He picked up the wand and waved it around, murmuring words that sounded like a spell was being cast.

"Don't point that thing at me! I don't want to turn into a slug or a radish or something!" I joked.

"Uncle Ash, I want this wand! Can I get it?" He continued dancing around with it in the air, acting like a wizard himself.

"Well, you have been good. Let me think about it for a minute." I snapped a picture of it and sent it to Paityn, asking if he had anything like it and if she had purchased one for him yet.

He clutched the wand tightly in his hand while looking at some books about magic a few feet from where he had grabbed it. It looked like someone may have developed a new interest. My sister texted back telling me he didn't have one and said I could buy it.

"Guess what?" I asked him once I read her message. "Santa thinks you've been a good boy. I sent him a message to ask him and to make sure he wasn't already bringing you one, and he said that you've been an angel all year."

"I can get it? You'll buy it for me?" he asked me, his whole face glowing.

"Yes! I'll buy it. And I'll let you pick out a book too if you want. But they'll be your Christmas gifts. Okay?" I'd probably wrap a little something else for him to have under the tree, but I wanted him to know these were part of his presents. Paityn stressed to us over the years the importance of not spoiling him. She wanted him to be grateful for what he had, and I respected it. We grew up that way too.

He ran to me, hugging my legs, thanking me, still holding on tightly to the wand. It felt good to be able to make him so happy after everything he'd been through lately. I encouraged him to select a book, and he chose one about the art of witchcraft and wizardry.

"Do you see anything you like in here?" I directed my attention back to Sidney, remembering that I needed an idea for his gift.

"Actually, yes," he answered, locking his eyes with mine. "I'm looking at it." I couldn't help the giant smile that curved up my cheeks. Maybe I'd just wrap myself in a big bow. That'd be both cute and funny, right?

"Ditto," I said, almost speechless. I took a beat, not knowing where to look. I glanced over at Liam and then back at Sidney. "We can talk more about that later. But seriously, do you see anything else you might like?"

"I've always been into wizardry myself," Sidney shared, picking up a wand identical to Liam's. "Maybe you could get me one too, and I'll use it to make my wish come true."

It became very clear that it was time to get out of here and get my nephew home to bed so I could have a few minutes alone with this guy.

"Done! I'll go pay for both wands and the book. You two can wait for me outside and enjoy the lights a little longer before we head home," I told them, grabbing the items and ushering them to the doorway.

TWENTY MINUTES LATER, we were back at the house, and Liam was changing into his pajamas and brushing his teeth. We tucked him into bed, since my mom and Paityn were still out.

With my dad already asleep, I was able to have some privacy with Sidney. I showed him my bedroom, the place I had slept my entire life, with the exception of the two years I was away in Nashville. I figured it was important for him to get a sense of who I was based on my possessions and the environment I chose to surround myself with. You could tell a lot about someone from their bedroom.

"You have a lot of stuff here," he said. "Hoarder much?"

"Very funny. Yes, I guess you can say I have a hard time letting go of things," I replied, picking up the baseball from my shelf that I'd had since middle school.

"I'm just joking. I love that you save things. It shows a sentimental side of you." He looked around at all of the pictures I had and then paused when he got to a framed photo of me with Sophia, Raelyn, Kendal, and Owen on my twenty-first birthday in Atlantic City. "This is a good shot!"

"Thanks! It was my favorite from the night. Well, it's probably my favorite from that entire weekend."

"Yeah? Tell me about it." Sideny sat down on my bed, still holding the frame in his hands.

"Owen's dad has a boat in Longport, New Jersey. Sophia wanted to check it out with Owen, and they figured since my birthday was coming, we could make plans to stay at the boat one night and then drive over to Atlantic City, which is only a twenty minute drive from the marina. I had an ulterior motive for wanting to go though." I took a deep breath, preparing myself to explain the sordid tale of how I was hoping to meet up with *Kira*. I hadn't shared any of that with him up to this point. "I was talking to someone online who claimed they were going to college at Stockton University."

"Claimed? What do you mean?" He put the picture down on the bed and brought his full attention to my face.

"Well... it turns out I got catfished actually." I watched his eyes for a reaction. But instead, there was nothing. No judgement, no laughter. Just genuine interest. So I continued, "I thought I was talking to a girl named Kira that lived out there, and I made plans to meet her at the casino. But she never came. And everyone else tried their best to make sure I still had a really good night, with a lot of success, I have to say. It was fun, and I keep that photo out to remind me of not only the amazing time I had with all of them that weekend, but to also help me stay true to myself."

"Doesn't it bring back memories of betrayal though?" Sidney asked me empathetically.

"One would think so, to be fair, but going through that experience woke me up in a way." I turned my body to face him to the left of me. "I found out the person pretending to be Kira was someone I already knew and saw pretty regularly. It was a guy named Louis who played in a band at the restaurant I was working at in town. He lied because he was afraid and insecure, and he wasn't confident enough to present who he was."

"That's super accepting and understanding of you to

see his perspective and what he was going through. I admire that." Sidney scooted closer to me on the bed.

"Well, it wasn't that difficult for me to put myself in his shoes. It took me a long time to accept who I was. And that situation made me realize I had to feel comfortable with myself if I wanted others to be."

"Ashton James, the more I learn about you, the more I fall for you."

Did he... Did he just say he's falling for me? Did that just happen? Pause.

"Wait. Can you repeat that?" I brought my body even closer to his. There was barely six inches of space between us now, and I could swear he was probably able to feel my heart pounding through my shirt. "I think I need you to say that to me again, but slower this time."

"Ashton, listen carefully. Every hour I spend with you has me more invested. I love how you carry yourself, and I love how you make me feel." There were three inches now. "And it's safe to say that I've been falling for you since the night you first introduced me to your family a few weeks ago."

"Is it okay that I started falling for you even before then?" I asked him softly, approaching his lips with mine.

"It's definitely okay, since I've been attracted to you since the first time I saw you," he whispered.

Zero inches now. It's happening.

He pulled me in, holding the back of my neck. And every ounce of my body felt the intensity. I pushed Sidney back lightly, moving myself with him as he fell into the pillows. We stopped only briefly to catch each other's stare and then picked up immediately, unable to resist the yearning between us.

It was the best ten minutes of my life up to this point.

Every second was perfection. And walking him downstairs, all I could think was that I wanted a repeat as soon as possible.

"Can I see you again soon?" he asked me when we finally said goodbye for the night. "I'll make myself available for you."

"Yes, very soon. Even if we have to fit something in between shifts," I replied, standing against his car with him, not wanting to go back inside.

"Maybe we can make time *during* our shifts. They have supply closets at the hospital, don't they?" he teased, stealing one more kiss before he opened his car door.

"We will definitely be hanging soon," I said. "Count on it."

"Bye, Ashton James. Try not to miss me too much."

I watched as he got into his front seat and secured his seatbelt. Then, I made myself turn to walk back toward the house, grinning the whole way.

I think I have a boyfriend.

We didn't say it, but based on all that transpired between us, I was pretty sure I did.

Wait until Sophia hears about this.

24

SOPHIA

Ladies night out was something all three of us needed. We even saw Paityn laugh a few times and truly enjoy herself, which we hadn't seen since before Bradley passed away. She was in for a long journey ahead, but I stood by the decision she made to come back home. It was the right move, both figuratively and literally.

When I made it home, Owen and Bowie were snuggled up in bed. I got undressed, slipped my silk pajama short set on, and climbed in to join them. Within minutes, the three of us were wrapped up in comfort together, and just as I was about to doze off, my phone alerted me with a text.

> Ashton: I have news. Tonight was
> AWESOME. I have a boyfriend. At least, I
> think I do. Call me when you can.

I gasped so loudly I had to cover my mouth before I woke anyone up. Ashton and Sidney were officially a thing! This was amazing! I texted him back saying I'd call in the morning and I couldn't wait to hear about it. My little brother deserved happiness. It was his time to experience a real love, one that he would either hold onto forever or grow so much just from having experienced it.

When the sun came up, Bowie wanted to eat and go out right away. Owen took care of that and let me rest a little since I was out the night before, but I didn't take advantage of it for too long. I sprang out of bed and into my slippers once I remembered Ashton's text. I had to know!

"Okay, spill it! Right now!" I exclaimed as soon as he picked up the FaceTime call.

"Did you even have coffee yet? You look like you just rolled out of bed."

"I did just roll out of bed. I haven't even made it to the kitchen yet." I took a brush and untangled my hair while on the line with him, and then I walked out to see Bowie lying at Owen's feet. He was at the stove with a spatula in his hand, cooking breakfast.

I really did marry the best guy ever.

"Oh, is Owen cooking? Can I come over?" Ashton asked once he saw the turkey bacon and eggs.

"That's fine, but get over here fast! I'm hungry, and I want the story!"

"I'll be there in fifteen minutes. Don't eat without me!"

I hung up and brewed some dark roast while we waited, and then I set the table for three. Sunday morning breakfast with two of my favorite guys after Saturday night drinks with two of my favorite girls made for a top notch weekend in my book.

By the time I finished my first cup of coffee, the doorbell was ringing, followed by a quick turning of the knob.

"I'm here! Everyone decent?" I heard Ashton say as he walked in.

"All good! Come to the kitchen," I yelled. And Bowie

ran out to get him and bring him back to us sitting at the table, her tail wagging with excitement.

"That's right, girl. The one you love most has arrived. Your dreams of seeing me again have come true!" he told her, petting her head as she settled along with him at his seat.

Owen stood up to get the food from the stove and put it onto plates in the middle of the table. My mouth began watering at the tasty aroma and delectable sight.

I scooped eggs onto my dish faster than I ever had in my life, while simultaneously prompting Ashton to fill us in. I had waited long enough to find out why he thought Sidney was his boyfriend now.

"Last night, after Mom and Paityn left the house to come get you, Sidney came over. He and I had made some plans to go to the village, but when I found out I was going to be watching Liam, I told him we would have to do it another night. He then said we could still go and bring the little guy, if that was okay with me and Paityn."

"Oh, okay. Yeah, Paityn mentioned that you were going into some stores and might buy Liam a gift, but I don't think I realized Sidney was with you," I replied.

"I ended up getting both of them a magic wand from The Cloak and Wand shop. I think they liked the idea that they'd have something to connect them too." Ashton shoveled some of the scrambled eggs into his mouth.

"So, I'm sure your new boyfriend loved seeing all of the lights, especially the tunnel, am I right?" He showed me some of the videos and pictures they took the night before on his phone.

"I'm hoping that's what he is," he spoke calmly, sipping his coffee. "I feel like we are exclusively dating, even though we haven't really said that."

"Well, what made you get there in your mind. Was it something he said?"

"He said a lot, and all of it was really nice, but it wasn't just that." He looked down at Bowie, avoiding eye contact with Owen and myself.

"Ashton, spill it! Tell me what happened!" I demanded, almost jumping across the table to him.

"Is it a good look if I kiss and tell?" he asked with a smirk, blushing a little.

"Wow, man, you guys kissed?" Owen asked, joining the conversation.

"We did kiss, for a while actually. And he might've told me he was falling for me." He paused, his face growing more flushed. "And I might've said it back."

"Look at you! Is that why you think you two might be serious now?" Owen followed up.

"Well, it was that and the way we left things, and it was really just the entire night and the vibe between us. I will definitely clarify with him as far as status goes, but I wanted to get your opinions on something." Ashton looked back and forth at our faces, waiting for confirmation.

"Of course! What is it?" I inquired, still so excited for him.

"Do you guys think I should tell Sidney about Kendal and I both being interested in him and how we kind of had a pact between us that we would let the other take a shot, so to speak? I mean, I almost feel like he should know that, but a part of me thinks it wasn't too big of a deal because we didn't make a bet or anything. We just gave each other space and time to try and hang with him to see who had the better connection."

"That is tricky. On one hand, you didn't really do anything wrong, since neither of you knew him, and you both had interest in finding out more about him. But on the other hand, if he found that out later, he might be upset that you never shared that piece of information with him." I honestly would be conflicted too on whether or not to say anything.

"I really don't want Kendal or Emily or anyone else to accidentally say something to him one day and it cause a problem. And I'd like to have full transparency in the relationship. I'd expect the same from him."

"I feel like it could be a light conversation that can be brought up while the two of you are hanging one night," Owen advised. "You can open the dialogue by saying you have a funny story and then fill him in on how both of you noticed him at the hospital and confided in each other that you'd like to find out more about him. He'll probably be flattered. I doubt he'd be mad."

"Owen's right, Ash. Do it that way. But don't hide it. It will just sit and loom over you like a secret you are keeping from him, and then it will make you anxious and stressed out."

"I will have to figure out the right moment." He picked up his coffee mug, drank the rest, and then refilled. "I appreciate you guys."

"Try and do it before Christmas so you can relax and enjoy the holiday with everyone and not have it on your mind," I told him just before filling my mouth with the rest of the soft, fluffy eggs on my plate, followed by the last slice of crispy turkey bacon.

So good!

"I definitely will." Ashton sat back comfortably in his chair, putting his right leg up over his left, giving the impression he was staying a while. "Can you believe how fast it came this year? I'm still not done with my shopping."

"It crept up for sure, and I'm with you on the shopping. But I feel like we really have to make this year great for Paityn and Liam." I poured myself and Owen some more coffee. "This will be their first Christmas without Bradley."

"Whatever you and your family need, I'm there," Owen offered. "I know this is going to be hard on them."

"Maybe we can make some ornaments with pictures of them with Brad, and they can hang them on our tree this year if they want but also keep them afterward," Ashton suggested.

"I like that idea!" I praised my brother. And then I had another thought. "What if we also put together a photo book for them of every Christmas they've had, including shots of Doug, and we can add in some new memories that we have over the final days leading up to the day this year?" I exclaimed.

"That sounds perfect! And I think we know a couple of photographers that could get the job done," Owen said with a smirk.

"Agreed! We have that part covered. We'll just have to collect some old photos. I'll see what Mom and Dad have and go through all of our Facebook accounts."

"Cool! And I'll pick up some really nice Christmas balls in town," Ashton volunteered.

We made our plan and vowed to set it into motion immediately. Realistically, there wasn't that much time left to make it happen. And I also wanted to chat with my nephew and see what role his dad played in making the holiday special for him. This way, I could make an effort to replicate at least one of them as a tribute to my late brother-in-law.

The first one without him there was going to hit hard, really hard, but that didn't mean we couldn't try and soften the blow with some reminders of what things were like when Bradley was here. The good part was that they always came back to Pennsylvania for Christmas to spend time with family, so my sister and Liam would still have that constant in their lives.

25

ASHTON

Robert Frost once said, "The afternoon knows what the morning never suspected." Boy, did the afternoon sure know today! And my morning was completely in the dark.

When I got into work, I had to get changed into my scrubs, so I went straight to the locker room after taking a peek at the schedule board. To my disappointment, I wasn't paired up with Sidney for this shift, but I at least knew he'd be at the hospital and that there'd be a chance of running into him.

Once I got myself ready for rounds, I shoved my things inside my locker and shut the door quickly. Zipping around the corner, I bumped into someone bent down tying their shoe.

"I'm so sorry. Please excuse me," I said before they could even stand up. "I'm in such a hurry because my shift starts in a few minutes."

"Not forgiven!" the familiar female voice blurted out to me. "Watch where you're going, little brother." Kendal smiled and gave me a little shove.

"Oh, hey!" I replied. "How's it going?" I feel like I haven't seen you in about a week."

"Yeah, I don't think we've been scheduled the same days. Things are good. Just about ready for the holidays." She looked down at her pants and shoes and started patting her clothes down with her hands, as if to iron out the wrinkles. "You?"

"I'm good. I don't know how much Sophia shared with you, but Paityn and Liam are home and staying at our house with me and my parents, so that's nice. And I think it was a good decision for them."

"Your sister did tell me that. I love that for all of you. I still can't believe Bradley's gone, but I know how close your whole family is and trust you'll be able to help each other through it."

"Thanks. I know it'll continue to be a process," I told her, edging my way toward the door. I had to clock in. I was such a rule follower, stressing about possibly being even a minute late.

"Everything else okay?" she asked before I could leave. I couldn't help but wonder if she was talking about Sidney. I didn't really want to tell her how amazing things had been between us. I felt like it'd be rubbing it in her face, and I didn't want to do that.

"Things are going well, yes. I can't complain." I hoped she'd leave it at that and not expect me to elaborate, but I was wrong.

"Are you and Sidney spending a lot of time together?"

"I guess you could say that." I drew my eyes from her and over to the door, implying I really needed to get going.

"Good! I'm glad you're happy. You deserve it." She ran her hands through her hair and looked down at her feet. "It's kind of crazy that we both had a thing for him, isn't it?

Does he even know about that? Does he care that we had a deal between us?"

"I don't know if I would call it a deal. But he doesn't know yet. I'm planning on telling him all about it soon though." The door creaked behind me, and Kendals eyes grew large.

"Hey, you! Long time, no talk!" she said to whoever was standing behind me.

Just then, I turned around to find, not just someone from the hospital overhearing the tail end of our conversation, but the only person I wouldn't have wanted to hear. I really wished Kendal could've just left the conversation after a few pleasantries.

Why does Sidney have to show up right now?

"What's this deal the two of you were talking about? Clue me in." He walked further into the room, now standing only two feet from me.

"I'm not sure exactly what you heard, but there wasn't really a deal. I was actually just correcting Kendal's use of the word because it wasn't like that at all," I tried to explain.

"Yeah, it wasn't a deal. It was more like an agreement or an understanding, if you will." She made an effort to clear things up and then headed toward the door he just came through. "I feel like I should let you two talk about this." And then she was gone.

"What does she mean that you two had an understanding? About me? What kind of understanding?" he asked me once the door was shut again. I could tell by the way his arms were crossed that he was annoyed.

"I was planning to tell you the story. I just didn't know how to bring it up," I told him, moving closer. "It's not what you think. We both just had an interest in you and wanted to hang out with you. Neither of us knew if you were single or straight or where you were from or what you liked. We didn't know anything, so we agreed that we would each just try to get to know you in our own way."

"So the two of you had interest, told each other, and then just competed to see who could get my attention? Is that right?"

No. That's not right. Not really.

"You're taking it the wrong way!" I exclaimed with fear in my voice. "We weren't competing for you. It wasn't like a bet. We just both thought you seemed like an incredible guy and didn't want to stake a claim. Her and I have been close for a long time, as you know. We wanted to go about it in a fair way."

"It doesn't feel very fair to me, if I'm being honest. It feels shady, like you were keeping something from me this whole time. And what? Did she concede when she saw she wasn't getting anywhere?" His eyes filled up with frustration and pain.

"Sidney, it wasn't like that. I swear to you it wasn't. It was all very above board. We were completely open to the possibility that you could form a connection with either of us or neither of us."

"I don't know, Ash. I think I should've found this out before now. To me, it sounds like a pact was made between two friends who had some fun going after what they wanted."

"We weren't doing anything for fun. I liked you, and so did she. But we were leaving it up to you and leaving it to what was meant to be. There was no guarantee you'd hit it off with me or with her." I attempted to hold his hand, but he wasn't very receptive. He let me grab it for a few seconds and then pulled it away.

"How did the conversation go when you and I were

getting closer? Did you just tell her you got the guy?" He searched my face for clarity.

"No! Nothing like that!" My eyes began to fill now. "I didn't have to tell her that. She saw we had something real and said she was done trying to pursue you. That's all! And she's fine. Kendal and I are fine."

"Well, it's good you didn't let someone like me ruin your relationship. I'm not worth it." He wiped a tear from his face.

At this point, I realized I would definitely be late clocking in for my shift, but I didn't care. If it took five more minutes, or even twenty, I needed him to see we were just being respectful to each other.

But were we respectful to him?

"I'm so sorry for not saying something to you sooner about this. I didn't realize until recently that you had feelings for me. Up until then, I thought there was still a chance I might lose whatever it is that we have. And bringing this up didn't feel right. I'm seriously very sorry."

"Listen, we both have to get working." He made his way over to the door and grabbed the knob. "I need some space from this situation."

I froze. He left. And I stood there, not knowing what to think or how to feel.

He had every right to be upset at the thought of me keeping something from him, but it just really wasn't as bad as what he was thinking. Kendal and I weren't doing anything malicious. On the contrary, we were being mindful of each other's feelings. This wasn't a game to either of us.

How do I make him see that?

THE REST of my shift was spent trying to stay focused on the job and nothing else, but every so often, small glimpses of Sidney walking out of the locker room crept into my mind. I couldn't wait to get out of the hospital and home to my bed, where I always did the best reflection.

When I finally rested my body under my blankets, I felt a sense of relief mixed in with delayed panic. I was alone with my thoughts and could really make an effort to formulate a plan of action, but fear was consuming me. There was a very strong chance that I would lose the greatest connection I had felt up to this point in my life. It could all be over, just like that. And I would have significant regret.

But I can't let it happen.

I searched my brain for explanations, but nothing I came up with was any different from what I already told him. He didn't seem to want to hear what I had to say, and he certainly didn't seem to believe me.

So how do I make him see that all of it was innocent and that we wanted him to be the one to decide who he had something with, if it was even between myself and Kendal?

About an hour passed by, where I was tossing and turning, trying to think of what I could do to show him how much he meant to me and what an incredible impact he had already made on my life. I thought about our first date and the first time he met my family, as well as our first kiss, and I thought about our last kiss. It seemed like I would pass out from exercising my brain for so long, when it finally occurred to me what I needed to do.

Instead of continuing to explain or give excuses for the way I went about things, I needed to completely own up to the role I played in making him feel hurt and deceived. Taking responsibility for your actions is the first step in showing someone you care. And I did care, a lot.

I had to tell the truth, apologize again, and express my acknowledgement of the way he was feeling. I then had to offer to make amends and to not allow something like that to ever happen again, and then I had to follow through. It was also necessary to let him know how important he had become to me.

I decided I was going to write him out a very heartfelt text message. I didn't want to let too much time go by before reaching out to him, but I also wanted him to know that if he needed more space, I was going to respect that. Below was what I sent:

MY CELL: Sidney, I hope you don't mind hearing from me at this time, but I don't like how we left things, and all I can do now is think about you. I'm not going to keep explaining my side of things or justify the intentions that Kendal and I had. Instead, I am going to take accountability. As soon as I started to get close to you, I should have told you that both of us had been interested and that we had shared that with each other. You had every right to know that she and I agreed to let the other pursue you. I can absolutely see why finding that out the way you did made you upset and made you feel like we were, or I was, keeping it from you.

Moving forward, if you'll still have me, I promise to never make a similar mistake again. I'll be transparent in all aspects, and you won't ever have to doubt your trust in me. You have my word. Like I said, that's only if I'm lucky enough to remain on this journey with you and see where things go. My relationship with you makes me happy, so I'm praying you'll find it in you to forgive me. I understand if you need more time and space, and I will respect that as long as you wish. When you are ready, assuming you will be ready, I'd like to talk with you and see if we can move on, together.

After I saw the message was delivered, I waited with my phone in my hand for a little while, in case he read it and felt the desire to text back or call me. He didn't. But that was okay. There was no guarantee he had even seen it yet, and even if he did, he may not have wanted to respond too quickly. His need to process was more important than my need to feel better. So, I would wait. I'd wait as long as I had to. I just hoped he could see how much I cared and how much I truly didn't want to lose him. I could see a real future with this guy, and I prayed he could see one with me.

26

SOPHIA

C hristmas was just a few days away. I felt prepared as far as the gift buying went, but I knew I'd need to hit the grocery store at least one more time. Our traditional Feast of the Seven Fishes was a big deal, and we were going to be contributing to two different meals on Christmas Day. Thankfully, Mom and Paityn had breakfast taken care of. But Owen and I had to split our afternoon and evening between my family and his.

We weren't quite ready for celebrations just yet though. James Taylor Photography still had two more jobs to do and a consultation before we could call it quits for the holiday break. One was an engagement shoot, and the couple wanted the shots electronically sent to them within forty-eight hours so they could make the announcement on social media on Christmas Day. The other was a holiday party in New Hope for a real estate company, and that one was tonight.

Owen and I were hired to capture highlights from the event, including speeches, toasts, menu options, and individual shots of specific agents. The company planned to update their website in the new year with their favorites from the night. And even though we were the photographers, I still felt the need to dress up. I wore a black dress with black heels and added a silver clutch with silver jewelry. I wore my hair down and curly with light makeup. Owen wore a black suit with a white button-down shirt and shiny black shoes, hair pushed back.

We look the part.

The man who hired us had been an executive for years. He grew up in Bucks County and always dreamed of being part of a business like this since he was in high school. As soon as he graduated, he immediately went for his real estate license and kept going.

He asked us to start thirty minutes early with taking pictures of the venue and the guests entering. We were told this was the best time to get individual photos, since many people would be having drinks soon after, and we were given a list of names with images included to help us identify our targets. They were also given a heads-up to introduce themselves to us upon arrival.

Over the course of three hours, we met several well-established realtors and their significant others, as well as various others who worked for the company. The food was displayed beautifully, which made our job easy there, and the lighting was almost perfect, which assisted us in nailing the angles for the speeches and toasts.

It was really a great night, and the guests were genuinely enjoying themselves. I loved that coworkers had the opportunity to unwind and interact socially at the end of each year to celebrate their successes and the holiday season. It was very nice to see everyone so happy, clinking glasses, laughing at each other's jokes and stories, and tearing up the dance floor.

They can ask us back to do this every year until we retire.

As the night came to a close, we began packing up our equipment and extending well wishes to anyone who passed by. One guest stopped to chat for a few minutes, wanting to know if we lived in the area and if we were in the market for a new home.

Well, coincidentally, we are sir. What do you have available?

We shared with him the kind of place we were looking for, and he took our contact information, saying he would send us an email with what potential listings he knew of.

Dare I get hopeful? Not yet. I'll do that when we are actually going to see a place we might like. Until then, I pray.

THE NEXT MORNING, after some coffee and showers, Owen logged onto his computer to check if he had received anything from the realtor we met at the party. I figured it was too soon to hear anything, especially given the season, but to my surprise, I was wrong.

The agent had sent over a listing for a house in our price range, and it was modern and chic. It was listed a couple of weeks back, and I was honestly surprised it hadn't been snatched up. From the photos, it looked striking, but not so much that it didn't seem realistic. It had three bedrooms and two and a half bathrooms. It was located only five minutes away from our current residence, and it had been built within the last fifteen years. The only negative I could see from its online description was that it did not have a yard.

"Owen, I really want Bowie to have space to run around in, and we need an outdoor landscape for shoots, where we can plant some small trees or bushes and a variety of flowers," I told him as we both checked out the property on his computer.

"I agree," he responded. "If we're going to move, it should be a decent upgrade, and it should help us improve our personal and professional life."

"Can you let the agent know that this one isn't for us and that we'd be interested in hearing about other listings in the area that match our desires?" I asked him.

"I'll do that now," he said, opening up the reply to the message the realtor sent. "Try not to worry. We'll find something that's perfect for us."

Over the next couple of hours, Owen refreshed his email repeatedly, impatiently waiting for a response. And each time he checked, he let out a sigh of disappointment. It seemed like a lot of time had passed, but it hadn't reached eleven o'clock in the morning yet, and we just met the guy the night before. Oddly enough, *I* was the one telling *him* that we had to trust the process.

Just before noon, while we were organizing client folders in the studio, an alert came through.

Please let that be a new house update.

Owen walked over to check his email, and when he clicked on his inbox, his brows rose in delight. I knew we'd hear from the realtor soon enough. I was at his side in seconds to get a glimpse at what was sent over. It was a house about ten minutes away, according to Google Maps, but the weird part was it was an address inside Peace Valley Park.

"Where did this listing come from?" I asked Owen, still trying to make sense of it. "This house is located at the lake?"

Our lake? This can't be real. There must be some kind of mistake.

We had already done a search online for homes for sale in our area, and when we specifically put in Peace Valley Park, our search turned up nothing.

"I don't know, Soph, but this looks legit," Owen said, scrolling through the photos of the house on his laptop. "This place is rustic but with some newer renovations in the last five years. It's a good size, and it was just put on the market this week."

"I can't believe there's actually a house for sale at the lake," I replied, bending down to look with him. "It's quite lovely. Do you think this is an accurate representation?"

"I know what you mean. Sometimes the person taking the photos uses different perspectives to make the rooms look larger than they are. It's possible that was done here." Owen grabbed his phone from the desk.

"Are you going to contact the realtor again?" I asked curiously. "I'd like to see the house in person as soon as possible."

"You read my mind! That's exactly what I'm doing. He may know of an upcoming showing."

"That would be amazing! The location has me, and the price is right for us, but this virtual tour isn't enough for us to make a decision. We need to physically walk through the property."

"Agreed! And if we like what we see, we may put in an offer soon?" he asked me, pulling me close to him for a side hug.

"Maybe? No. Definitely! I'm in if you are. But let's temper our expectations until we see it for ourselves. I think we both know well enough the magic of good photography and even better editing," I joked, trying to tell myself more than Owen to not get too excited just yet.

Within ten minutes, the realtor responded to the text

Owen had sent to the number provided in the email. He said he had some free time late this afternoon to take us over and look at the house.

What? Today? Really?

Late afternoon would work because we had the engagement photo scheduled, but it wasn't until later, just before sunset. Our plan was to take the pictures at a nearby farm, since they were going with a country theme for their wedding, and then go home to work on the edits right away. The sooner we had the package completed and sent over to the couple, the sooner we were able to start our break and fully begin celebrating Christmas. And Oliver and Chloe were flying into town the day after tomorrow, so I really wanted this assignment out of the way before then.

Owen told the agent we'd meet him at the house at three o'clock. I still felt like it might be too good to be true. I halfway expected to wake up from a dream any second now. But I pinched myself, and nothing happened.

I'm awake. And our dreams of living at our happy place might come true.

BOWIE WANTED to come for the ride, especially when she heard us talking about the lake, but we thought it might be best to do the tour of the house without her. If we fell in love with it, made an offer, and had it accepted, then we'd take her over to check out the new digs. It turned out our favorite place had become her favorite place too.

We got a treat and lured her into her crate, just as we always did when she was home alone. There was some soft whimpering, but we promised her we'd be back soon. She could've made the argument that it would be fine for her to come along and just stay in the car with the windows down until we were done, and then we could take her for a walk. But I didn't think it was right to leave a dog in the car like that for more than a few minutes. There could be questions and conversation that kept us busy for a while, and that wasn't fair.

"Do you think this will be it?" I asked Owen once we were driving. "Do you think this is the one?"

"I'm very optimistic, Sophia. I'm keeping my fingers and toes crossed!"

"It's a good thing I'm driving then I guess!" I joked, glancing over at him in the passenger seat.

We pulled into the soft gravel driveway, parked behind the real estate agent, and viewed the stunning house resting just beyond the lake. It had wooden beams that were warm and golden in the afternoon sun. The roof was steep and dark, framed with stone chimneys that promised cozy fires inside. Wide windows reflected the sparkle of the water, and a wraparound porch stretched lazily along the front, dotted with rocking chairs and soft lantern light that was just beginning to glow. The lake shimmered behind it, calm and glassy, catching every cloud and color of the sky. A small dock jutted out into the water, with a canoe bobbing gently at its side.

"Owen, I think this might be the one. Are you seeing what I'm seeing?"

"I sure am! Wow! It's way better in person. Let's just hope the inside can meet our expectations."

The realtor greeted us at the front door and welcomed us in. He wore a relaxed, casual smile, clearly proud of this place and himself for being the one to potentially sell it. The moment we crossed the threshold, the scents hit us: cedar, fresh linen, a hint of something sweet like vanilla or baked apples. The entryway was bright and airy, with tall ceilings and natural light pouring in through skylights. The floors were lined with cherry hardwood.

To the right, a spacious living room opened up, anchored by a perfectly designed fireplace. The flames weren't lit, but we could easily imagine them crackling away on a chilly evening. Floor-to-ceiling windows lined the lake-facing wall, framing a view so perfect it could be a painting —calm water, trees swaying gently, maybe even a loon drifting by.

The realtor led the way as he narrated, his voice light and conversational, pointing out the reclaimed wood beams overhead, the subtle details in the trim, the built-in shelves tucked into unexpected corners. He took us into the kitchen, where everything gleamed. It was filled with marble counters and a farmhouse sink beneath a window that looked out onto the dock.

Every room really felt like it belonged in a magazine, but somehow not in an untouchable way. It was just as it looked in the pictures online, only better. It was calm. It was the kind of place where you could imagine waking up to birdsong, making coffee barefoot, opening the doors and letting the breeze drift through.

The realtor glanced back at us with a knowing smile, "Feels like home already, doesn't it?"

And honestly... it kind of does.

ON THE DRIVE HOME, we decided we were going to make an offer. It was right in our budget, and we loved it! There was no question that the house was right for us, and we wanted to snatch it up before anyone else did. Owen suggested we go a bit above the asking price to try and solidify the deal, and I was on board with that.

We have to have this house!

By the time we got back to our apartment and took care of Bowie, we only had about thirty minutes before we had to head back out to do the engagement photo shoot for the couple at the farm location, so the paperwork for the offer would have to be done afterwards.

But we were doing it. And within a couple of days, we could be finding out whether or not our dreams of having a forever home at the lake would come true.

God, please let us live at our happy place.

27

ASHTON

Sidney had to have read the text message by now. I sent it the night before last. He read it and was choosing not to respond to it. Maybe he needed more time to think about things, or maybe he just wanted to speak to me in person and was planning out exactly what he wanted to say to me. Either way, the not knowing was making me crazy. Though I told him I would respect his need for space, on the inside, I was dying. I wanted to make things right with him and continue exploring what we had between us. I needed him to see how much I cared.

I only had to work one shift over the next five days because I requested some time off for the holiday and because Oliver and Chloe were coming into town tomorrow. This meant I had only one opportunity to see Sidney at the hospital. I knew he could always show up at the house too or contact me to ask me to meet him somewhere, but I wasn't counting on either of those things to happen.

The bad news was that shift was three days away, and it was Christmas Eve Eve now. I couldn't wake up on

Christmas morning feeling the way I did. I just couldn't. I needed to do something.

Usually, I would call Sophia and ask her for help. She was definitely my go-to person when I was feeling low or stressed. But I didn't want to always be relying on my big sister for everything. At some point, I was going to have to figure out how to handle difficult situations on my own. Besides, I wasn't sure she would be able to give me advice on digging myself out of this.

Sidney was going to understand and forgive, or he wasn't, and I knew that. I also knew that sometimes just taking time to yourself gave you perspective. The problem was that I didn't want us to go through this holiday not speaking to each other. And my gut was telling me that I might still be able to do something before it was too late.

I decided I should do a heartfelt gesture to show him I was serious about him, that it was never a game or a competition, and that I truly was beginning to care for him in a way I never had about anyone before. I knew Kendal had work at the hospital tonight, doing one of her twelve hour shifts, so I texted her to ask if Sidney was on the schedule as well. If he wasn't there, then it was safe to assume he might be home, unless of course, he had already started talking to someone else and was out with them.

He is very good-looking, and sweet, and smart, and... who am I kidding? Anyone would be a fool not to be interested in a guy like him if they were single.

But it hadn't been that long since that day in the locker room, where things felt like they were crashing down. It was highly likely that nobody else had shown interest in the last week, and even if they had, it didn't mean he was also interested. I had to try and stay calm and focused, and I had to keep the faith alive.

Kendal: Hey! He worked a 12 hour shift
and finished this morning at 7, but he's not
working tonight or the next couple nights.
Next time he is here is the day after
Christmas. Hope all works out between the
two of you. Please keep me posted!

That made me feel a little bit better. Since he worked a twelve hour seven to seven shift, that meant he was probably sleeping all day today. If he saw the message yesterday morning or late the night before, he may have wanted to just sit with it for a bit but then had to go into work.

Yes. That is what I'm going with. That's why he hasn't texted or called me. I still have a chance to fix this. And I'm going to.

He wasn't at work, so I decided I would just go to his place to see him. Love apparently made you do crazy things. And before I could talk myself out of it, I grabbed my keys, threw on my coat, and headed out the front door.

ON MY WAY to his apartment, I made a quick stop to grab one of his favorite wines, something I learned from our night at the vineyard. I thought about what I would say if he was home and what I would do if he wasn't. I knew that if I knocked on his door and he answered, I would immediately tell him how sorry I was and express my feelings to him the best I could. If he wasn't home, I was going to wait. I'd wait as long as possible for him to come back home. I had to show him how important all of this was to me, how important he was to me.

I parked in the front lot outside of his building, looking for his car when I got out of mine. I didn't see it, but that was not a guarantee he wasn't home. He could've parked in the back lot or on the side somewhere. I held onto hope as I walked up the stairs to his floor and approached the door.

Please be here. And please don't have anyone else over. Please.

I knocked softly, the bottle of wine clutched against my coat. Thankfully, there was no peephole, so he wouldn't have been able to pretend he wasn't there if he saw it was me and didn't want to talk.

The door opened slowly, and he stood there in comfy red and green striped pajama pants with a white tee and cozy red socks.

How festive! Wow. And how cute!

I stared for a few seconds and then finally spoke, praying I didn't stumble over my words.

"Sidney, I am so sorry. I can't apologize enough to you, and I know saying that I'm sorry doesn't change how things happened, but I want you to know how regretful I am for keeping you in the dark and for making you feel like we were competing for your affection. We weren't, and I can assure you of that."

He listened and remained quiet, even after I was done speaking. He took a deep breath and let it out, and then he finally responded.

"Do you want to come in? It's freezing out there."

Yes. Please.

I walked into his apartment, handing him the bottle of wine after he closed the door behind me. "I brought this for you. Maybe we could have a glass together and talk a bit?"

"You remembered I liked the holiday red? Did you go back to the vineyard to get it?" He asked, analyzing the label on the bottle.

"Of course, I remembered. But no, I didn't have to go

back. The local wine and spirits place carries the same one. When I saw it, I felt like it was some sort of sign," I told him.

"Oh yeah? What kind of sign?" he asked me, grabbing two goblets from his cabinet.

"I don't know," I said casually, taking a seat on the right side of his small couch. "I guess I thought it was maybe a sign that I'd have an opportunity to set things right with you or that we would be okay. Was that just wishful thinking?"

"I'm leaning on the side of you being correct about the wine selection and it being a sign." He brought the bottle and the glasses over to his coffee table in front of the couch, sat down to the left of me, and began to pour. "The truth is, I was planning on reaching out to you either tonight or tomorrow morning." He handed me my glass and then picked his up, tipping it lightly into mine. "I actually tried to construct a response to your very well-worded message. I tried a few times if I'm being honest, but nothing I wrote seemed right. So, I thought the best thing would be to contact you and ask if we could meet in person to grab coffee or something. But here you are. It's like you read my mind."

"I think we are a little bit connected. At least, I'd like to believe so. And I really do appreciate you asking me to come in and being willing to talk with me." It felt good to know he was going to meet with me even if I hadn't shown up at his place.

He smiled and sipped more of his wine. "Listen, I should probably tell you that I did think there was some-thing not quite right about you and Kendal both showing interest in me, considering the two of you are so close. I wondered if each of you knew the other was flirting or trying to spend time with me, but I didn't want to say anything to either of you and cause a conflict."

"How long was it obvious that I was into you?" I asked him, taking a sip from my own glass.

"I'd say from the early stages of our outings," he responded sincerely. "But I was into you by then too, to be fair."

"Well, yeah, Kendal and I would never do anything behind each other's backs. She's like a sister to me. I swear, it was all on the up and up. We just both had the interest and didn't know what your preferences were or if you were single or even looking. She and I talked about it and decided the best approach would be for each of us to spend time with you on our own and get to know you and see if either of us connected with you. We also knew there was a chance neither of us would. And I was fully prepared to find out you were straight and very much attracted to Kendal. She's beautiful and witty and super fun. I wouldn't have blamed you, and I couldn't be upset if a guy I liked didn't... well, date guys." I shrugged my shoulders and placed my wine down on the table.

"So, you must've been pretty annoyed when she and Emily showed up at the bar that first night we went out, huh?" he asked me, knowing he was the one behind that particular surprise.

"I have to admit I was having a much better time with you before they arrived and made me share you. I went with it though and figured it would allow me to observe if you had any sparks flying with Kendal, or even with Emily for that matter. If you remember, I still didn't know at that point that you were interested in both men and women."

"Well, I didn't know you were inviting me to come out with you in the form of a date. I just thought we were hanging as co-workers. That's why I told the girls to join us for a drink." He scooted closer to me, leaving less than a foot between us. "I'm really sorry about that, by the way."

"I asked you to go out again soon after that, didn't I? I clearly wasn't too upset with you," I teased as I slid my left hand onto his right knee.

"I'm really glad you did," he answered, placing his right hand on top of my hand that was now working its way upward. Suddenly, the room seemed fifteen degrees warmer, and I felt my cheeks flush with heat.

"You know, since we are being completely transparent with each other, I want you to tell me something. Were you ever into Kendal at all? Or was that strictly just coworker and friend vibes?"

"Ashton, don't get me wrong... she's great, and we definitely have a nice friendship, but I didn't feel anything when I was with her, not like I do when I'm with you." He turned his head to lock eyes with me, and seconds later, his lips were locking with mine as well.

Thank God!

We kissed like it was our first time. I guess it's true what people say about making up after an argument and things being really hot. I slipped my right hand under his shirt to run my fingers up his stomach to settle on his chest. The intensity of our kiss grew more powerful, and I wasn't pulling away anytime soon. He could keep me in his arms all night if he wanted to.

When we stopped to get some air, he kept his eyes on my mouth and ran his hand through my hair, the way he knew I loved it.

With sultry eyes and an adorable smile, he asked, "Would you want to hang out for a while and watch a movie? You can stay over if you want."

Just when I'm thinking this night can't get any better, it does.

"I'd love to watch a movie with you." I poured more wine into my glass and into his. "And we can see where the night takes us," I replied playfully.

I can't just let him think he can have whatever he wants.

"Deal! What kind of film do you feel like watching?" he asked me, now holding the remote. "Rom-com?"

"Definitely a rom-com, but I'll let you pick!" It was his place, and I was the one who came here praying for forgiveness. Plus, I trusted his judgement.

He likes me after all.

"I think I'd like to watch a Christmas flick if that's okay. 'Tis the season and all that, right?" He surfed through the streaming services on his television.

"That's it!" I exclaimed when he landed on a movie I knew and loved. "That one right there! *Single All The Way!* It's amazing! Have you seen it?"

"I haven't yet, but with that level of excitement, it sounds like the winner."

He hit play on the screen with the remote and then placed it back down on the table. He retrieved a soft knitted blanket from a basket beside the couch and unfolded it, sitting back down next to me. He spread the blanket out over top of us and nuzzled in. I followed suit and wrapped my body in his. The movie started, but we didn't notice. In fact, I don't think we saw even one minute.

28

SOPHIA

"Oli and Chloe will be here in two hours!" I exclaimed when I got out of the shower on Christmas Eve morning. Bowie came running into the bedroom with her tail wagging and a purple squeaky ball in her mouth. I was sure she had no idea what I was talking about, but she could tell by my tone that it was something to be happy about.

"After you get yourself ready, we can head over. I'll take Bowie out one more time before we go," Owen said as he came into the room too. He had already taken his shower and was drinking coffee in the kitchen when I bellowed so loudly our neighbors could probably hear me.

Bowie would be coming with us for the nighttime portion of things, when we did our Feast of the Seven Fishes, but we were just going over to my parents' house for an hour or two to welcome in my older brother and his wife from California. I figured we should leave her home for that.

I blew out my hair and applied some foundation, mascara, and lip gloss. I put on a favorite pair of blue jeans, added a red sweater with baggy sleeves, and threw on my chestnut colored Uggs on top of socks that went halfway up my legs and were covered in snowflakes.

"Oli!" I yelled when we entered the kitchen and saw him sitting there with Chloe, my parents, Paityn, and Liam.

Where is Ashton? It's after eleven in the morning.

"Hey! How's it going, Soph? Miss me?" He stood up from his chair to give me a hug.

"Of course, I did! I know you two were home recently, but I always miss you!" I told him, locking him in for a warm embrace and then moving on to give some love to Chloe.

"My man!" Oliver said to Owen as he gave him a strong guy hug. "Has my sister been driving you crazy this holiday season?" He laughed, and I gave him the side eye.

"She sure does get into the spirit, but I've learned to love it. No complaints!" Owen responded wisely.

"Well, happy wife, happy life, right?" Oliver quipped back.

"Where's Ashton at? Doesn't he have off from work until the day after Christmas?" I asked the group, gazing around and toward the stairs, wondering if he was up in bed.

Although, I don't remember seeing his car outside.

"He texted me about a half hour ago to let me know he'd be home soon," Mom replied. "He stayed over at Sidney's last night. He said they were watching movies and fell asleep, and they were grabbing some breakfast this morning."

"Wow, Mom! You're okay with him sleeping at his boyfriend's house?" Oliver asked her with a smirk.

"Well, dear, he is an adult now. And are we calling Sidney his boyfriend? Have they made things official?" Mom looked at me, which I guess was fair.

I am the one he confides in.

"I think it's safe to assume, especially with him not coming home last night, that they are in fact a couple," I confirmed. "I know he was hoping for that after their last date anyway." I took my phone out of my purse and shot him a message.

> Me: Hurry and get home! I need details immediately.

For the next twenty minutes or so, we all got caught up on what had been going on out in California since we had last seen Oli and Chloe on the day of Bradley's funeral. They had Thanksgiving with Chloe's family, and they did some fun holiday outings throughout the month of December, including a work party for the hospital where my brother worked and a Santa bingo night at Chloe's school.

Paityn talked a bit about saying goodbye to her house and restaurant and what it had been like moving back here and trying to figure out life again. She seemed more positive about the future than she had been on the day she first came home with Liam and their moving truck, but it was still obvious she had a long way to go to fully heal.

"I think I'd like to open another restaurant at some point, but I'd want it to be something small, like a cafe maybe," Paityn told us. "The restaurant in Atlanta, as great as it was, brought a lot of stress to our lives."

"That sounds like a great idea!" Dad said enthusiastically. "I didn't know you wanted to do that." He sounded surprised, as if he had been worried she wouldn't find her way after losing her husband.

"I've been considering it over the last couple of weeks. But, Liam and I would need to stay here for a while, if that's okay. Renting out a new space and starting over in a new home might be too much to take on at one time." Paityn reached over to my nephew sitting in the chair next to her and brushed his hair lightly with her hand. She adored him, and I was so proud of how she continued to put him first in spite of how she was feeling.

"You and Liam can stay here for as long as you want, honey." My dad looked over at my mom, who was nodding along. "It's not like we don't have the room, and we enjoy having you both here every day."

My parents really did love having them at the house. Ashton was the only one staying here, and he wasn't home all that much. The two of them living in the basement was the perfect arrangement, and they could really benefit from being with family for a while.

"If you need help looking for a space to rent, I can give you the contact information for our realtor. We shared our preferences with the guy at a party we worked the other night, and by the next morning, he had a house to show us," Owen told my sister.

"Yes, please!" Paityn responded graciously. "Send the information to my phone as soon as you can. That'd be great!"

"And before anyone asks, we are still waiting to hear if our offer was accepted. As soon as we know, all of you will too," I announced. "We will show you pictures or perhaps bring you to see the house if we get it. Until then, we pray!"

My parents both did the sign of the cross on themselves, showing their way of sending us a blessing, and Liam did the prayer hands gesture with his eyes closed. I knew everyone else was hoping for the best, and that was really all I could ask for.

This is in God's hands now.

WHEN ASHTON FINALLY ARRIVED HOME, the group had dispersed to various locations. Paityn had taken Liam downstairs to feed Doug some hay, and my brother and Chloe had gone upstairs to settle in and rest before the evening's festivities. My parents both went to the grocery store to pick up last minute items for that evening and the next day. Owen and I were just about to make our exit.

"Wait! You guys can't leave yet," he insisted, noticing my handbag crossed over my body. "I have to tell you about last night!" Ashton had a huge smile on his face stretching from ear to ear.

I halted my steps toward the front door and turned around to go and sit down on the couch. Owen did the same. Bowie could wait just a little longer.

"We heard you slept over at Sidney's. Things must be going really well," I said, leading him into the story.

"Well, things actually weren't going well at all after he heard me talking with Kendal at work about how we both liked him and had an understanding. He showed up at the locker room in the hospital as we were wrapping up a conversation and got upset at what he thought had happened."

"Didn't you say you were going to tell him about all of that?" Owen asked.

"I was, but I hadn't had the chance. Then Kendal left, and I tried to explain everything, but he really wasn't having it. I waited and reached out later that night through text, apologizing and admitting I was wrong for not telling him sooner, but he didn't respond. So, last night, I decided I was going to pick up some wine and show up at his place to speak to him in person. I know it was bold, but I didn't want to go into the holiday on a bad note."

"Wow, Ash! I'm honestly so impressed with the way you handled yourself," I told him admirably.

"Thanks! And it worked out! I was prepared to have to wait for him, in case he wasn't home, but he was. He invited me in, and he opened the bottle I brought, and we sat down to have a glass together. He told me he didn't think texting back was the best and that he was going to reach out to try and meet up in person."

"This is great. I'm sure that made you feel good that he wanted to talk to you about it," Owen said.

"It did, yeah, and it made me care for him even more to see how forgiving and understanding he was being. So, we hung out some more, and he asked if I'd want to watch a movie. There was no way I was declining that. And he got a blanket, and we... we snuggled up and fell asleep watching *Single All the Way*." Ashton looked away as he ended that last sentence.

"You snuggled and fell asleep? Okay, sure. I'll pretend I believe you." I smiled and glanced over at Owen, who was also smiling, but in a proud brother kind of way. Ashton spoke no other words, but his face said he was in love. And I loved that for him.

IT WAS the night we'd all been waiting for: Christmas Eve and our traditional Feast of the Seven Fishes. We were all together, every last one of us, including both sets of grand-parents, Bowie, Mabel, and Doug. Cocktail hour had just begun, which meant that Elijah and Bethany joined us with Hope only minutes ago. Every year, like clockwork, they showed up just as the first toast of the night was about to be given. I swore my brother timed it that way on purpose.

Sidney wasn't here because he was spending Christmas Eve with his parents and waking up there on Christmas morning, but he planned to join us later in the day tomorrow. He didn't have much of a choice, now that he was dating a member of the James family. Holidays weren't exactly optional.

Kendal was stopping by tonight, but we'd see Raelyn and Kevin at Owen and Rae's parents tomorrow after mass. I was hoping now that Ashton and Sidney were a couple, there wouldn't be hard feelings between my little brother and Kendal. I know she said there wouldn't be, and she had always been like a part of our family, but she might still be upset that she didn't get the guy. Some people take that as a form of rejection, even though it really was based on a level of connection. I guess I was about to find out. The doorbell rang, and everyone on the guest list was accounted for, except for her.

"The party's here!" Kendal chanted as I opened the front door.

"Hey, girl! I'm so glad you could make it," I said, ushering her into the foyer. "Let me take your coat and hang it up."

"Oh, please! Stop it! I've been here enough to know where the closet is. I'll hang it."

"I always appreciate that you make time to come by each year. I'll have my dad make you something. Come to the kitchen!" I thought it would be better to get her a drink before she had to talk with Ashton again in person. They hadn't seen each other since that night at the hospital when Sidney walked in on their conversation.

"Hey, Daniel, Merry Christmas!" Kendal greeted my

dad so informally, the way she has for years. At this point, I was surprised she didn't just call him Dad.

"Thanks, Kendal! Get over here and give me a hug."

"Okay, I'll give you a hug, and you make me a drink. Deal?" she responded vivaciously. And he nodded and held his arms out to invite her in.

"Can you make me another one too?" I asked my dad once he began mixing.

"Sure thing! Where'd that husband of yours get off too?" Dad asked, probably wondering if Owen also needed a refill.

"He's with Ashton and Liam downstairs. Apparently, Liam taught Doug a new trick and wanted to show them." I didn't even know you could teach rabbits tricks until that little guy came into our lives.

"The bunny can do tricks? Like what?" Kendal asked, eyebrows raised in surprise.

"Well, I'm not sure what this new one is, but Liam has taught Doug to come to him and stand up on command. It's pretty wild to see," I told her.

"I need to see this for myself! Let's go down there." We grabbed our drinks and headed to the basement to find Liam kneeling down in front of Doug with a carrot.

"Spin! Spin, Doug! Spin!" Liam exclaimed.

"Has he gotten him to do it?" I asked, joining Owen and Ashton on the couch. Kendal sat down across from us on the small loveseat.

"Twice actually!" Ashton replied, seemingly impressed.

And just then, Doug spun around in a circle and stopped right where he began, waiting for his carrot.

"Wow! Liam, you're amazing!" I cried.

"No, Doug is amazing," he responded without missing a beat.

"That's so cool! You're doing such a great job with him!" Kendal said, leaning down to pat his back.

"Thanks! I'll teach him more too. One thing at a time is what Mom tells me."

"That's right. Your mom is a wise woman," I interjected, giving Paityn the praise she deserves.

"Hey, little brother!" Kendal addressed Ashton. "Where's lover boy?"

"Very funny," he responded sarcastically. "Sidney's with his parents tonight."

"Too bad! But all is good with you two now? Did you end up seeing him last night?" Kendal appeared genuinely interested in my brother's happiness, as I knew she would be. She really did love him as if he were her own family.

"Yes, I saw him. Thank you again for checking the schedule at work. It was a big help," Ashton started to share part of what happened, but I had a feeling he'd be mindful of Kendal's feelings and not go into too much detail. "I ended up going over to talk with him, and we were able to work things out and get back on track."

"That's awesome! I'm happy for you two." She took a sip from her drink, which happened to be a very delicious holiday martini. In the past, we've had chocolate and creamy concoctions, but my dad was being considerate of my new diet and made this year's cocktail a fruity blend. Not being able to have dairy was difficult, but I had to stay away from anything that would cause inflammation. "You know, you don't have to downplay things for me," Kendal spoke again. "I've moved on from the hot nurse. In fact, I have a date the day after tomorrow. So, don't worry about me."

"Cool! Yeah, I was just trying to be respectful. Things

are really good between us. He's coming over tomorrow evening for dinner," Ashton replied.

"I love that for you so much. You deserve it!" she said joyfully.

"I love that for you too!" I told him. "I can see you care a lot for this guy."

Ashton smiled and couldn't stop smiling. And my heart was full for him.

AFTER DINNER, all four of my grandparents had to get going. They hit the sack pretty early these days to wake up at the crack of dawn simply because they wanted to. I couldn't imagine ever feeling that way. And Liam and Hope were crashing out from too much excitement, so Paityn made them comfortable on the couch in the living room by tucking them in at separate corners with some red fleece blankets my parents had draped over the sides for an added festive touch.

The rest of us decided to play a game in the family room called *Same But Different*. Elijah and Bethany picked it up from the Five Below store near their house. The rules of the game were that every person took a turn selecting two cards from the piles in the center, one being a safe card and one being a risky card, and read it aloud to the group. There were two scenarios on the cards, and everyone had to say a phrase that would be applicable to both. The person reading from the card they chose then decided which phrase they liked the most and gave the card to whoever said it. At the end, the player with the most cards won.

We played that game for about an hour, and it was definitely one I would play again. I was laughing throughout most of it, especially when Chloe chose cards where we had to come up with a phrase that you would say to your gym teacher and something you would say on a first date.

"I'm not usually this sweaty!" Ashton shouted. And Chloe chose him as the winner, which was fair, since nothing anyone else said came close to being that funny.

"I'm glad you guys liked it," Elijah said. "There were at least thirty games to choose from, but this one stood out. I had a feeling our family would have some fun with it."

"Yeah, good call," Oliver replied. "I don't know how we can beat this tomorrow night."

"We have to try though. Sidney is coming, and I want him to have a good time," Ashton exclaimed.

"I'm sure we'll think of something," I assured him. "Don't worry about it."

"Excuse me a moment," Owen said, pulling his phone out of his pocket. "I have to take this."

I wonder who is calling him at this time on Christmas Eve that warrants him stepping away to talk.

"I should probably go in a minute. My parents want me over for breakfast in about twelve hours, and I haven't wrapped their gifts yet." Kendal grabbed her purse and stood up to say her goodbyes. She was making her way to the foyer closet to get her coat when Owen came back.

"I have wonderful news!" he blurted with elation.

"What is it? Who was on the phone?" I asked him.

"That was our realtor. He apologized for calling so late and on a holiday evening, but it was for a good reason." Owen moved to where I was now standing, preparing to walk Kendal out, and put his arms around my waist from behind me.

Oh my God. Did we get it?

"Ladies and gentlemen, our offer was accepted!" he proudly announced.

Everyone cheered and expressed their happiness for us in this moment. My eyes filled up with tears of joy as soon as the words left Owen's mouth. I couldn't believe it was happening, even though part of me had a feeling all of it was meant to be.

"It's really ours?" I asked him, wiping my face with the back of my hand.

He kissed me on my lips and helped dry my eyes. "Yes! And we will go to settlement in 30 days and can move in right after."

"That's incredible!" I exclaimed. "Although, we have to have him list our apartment and find someone to rent it too."

"You two will get all of that figured out," Oliver chimed in. "Enjoy the moment!"

"I'm so glad I didn't leave yet!" Kendal said. "I would've missed the big news in real time!" She hugged me tightly and then reached out for Owen to join in our embrace. "Congratulations! I can't wait for the housewarming party!"

It took another hour for it to settle in that we were going to be living at the lake. Over the years, it had become the one place we could go to find comfort and peace.

29

ASHTON

I woke up on Christmas morning smiling. It wasn't on the same level as the morning before, where I had woken up with Sidney, but I was very happy. It was Christmas, I had my whole family around me, and I was going to see my guy later on.

So why am I still in bed? Let's get this day started!

I quickly threw on my holiday pajamas that were given to me last night from *Santa*. Every year, we'd receive a new pair, and I would be okay if this continued the rest of existence. It was another one of our James family traditions that never got old. And Mabel waited patiently as I slid on my cozy white slippers, washed my face, brushed my teeth, and combed through my hair. Mom always took pictures of us opening gifts, so I had to look at least somewhat presentable.

When everyone was awake and accounted for and had some breakfast in them, we opened gifts. Thankfully, there was enough room in the house for the entire family to stay over and wake up together on our favorite holiday. Sophia and Owen stayed with Bowie in Sophia's old room. Oliver and Chloe took the guest room. Elijah and Bethany stayed in the loft area, while Hope stayed in the basement with Paityn, Liam, and Doug.

As in all years past, we started by having the youngest go first with receiving presents, and then we moved onto our sibling exchange once Mom and Dad had their turns. Things were coming to a close, and Oliver said he had one more gift to give out.

"This is from me and Chloe," he told us, handing everyone a black box with a ribbon tied at the top. "Everyone has to open it at the same time."

"Wow, the mystery, Oli! I'm barely able to handle the suspense," Sophia said, holding on tightly to her box.

Oliver gave one to my parents, one to Elijah and Bethany, one to Paityn, one to Sophia and Owen, and one to me. Liam and Hope sat with all of us, watching in anticipation.

"Are we doing it now? Is there a countdown?" I asked him jokingly.

"Yes! Everyone go ahead," he commanded. Chloe had her phone ready to record all of our reactions.

This is big news. I can feel it.

We all simultaneously untied the bows and removed them from the boxes. Then we lifted the tops of the boxes off to reveal a Christmas stocking. Oliver told us there was something inside the stocking, so each of us stuck our hands in to pull out the object.

Whoa!

"Oh my goodness, Oli! Chloe! Congratulations!" Sophia shouted.

"The two of you must be over the moon," Paityn exclaimed.

"We are very excited. Thank you," Chloe replied with a glow.

The item inside the stocking was a photograph of a sonogram. Chloe was pregnant! Our family was being blessed with another baby.

And we really need this after losing Bradley so recently.

"Wait, there's more. Look closely at the sonogram. Do you see it?" Oliver asked the group and waited, a sly grin painted on his face.

"It's twins?" I asked in surprise. "You guys are having twins?"

"You are kidding!" My dad said with skepticism in his voice.

"It's true! Chloe is pregnant, with two boys. She's due in May."

I can't really believe this. Two baby boys? Wow. This is wild.

My mom, with tears in her eyes, offered hugs and kisses to both Oliver and Chloe, repeatedly telling them how fortunate she felt to be a grandmother again and wishing them the best with the pregnancy. She even told them she'd fly out there and help them when the babies arrived, as they were sure to have their hands full. Of course, all of us were going to want to be there when they came into this world.

Elijah and Bethany said they'd give them anything they still had from when Hope was born that wasn't just for girls, like a stroller and crib and things of that nature that they'd kept in the attic in case anyone would need it in the future.

And here we are.

I couldn't wait to share the news with Sidney. In fact, I realized at that moment that whenever something big happened in my life, I wanted to immediately tell him about it. I never felt like that before with anyone else, not even when Riley and I had become close friends or when I thought I was getting really close with *Kira*. It was different this time. Sidney was different.

THE REST of the morning was spent relishing in the idea of having twins in the family. Liam was euphoric about having more boys, and Hope was trying to process her not being the baby anymore. Both of them vowed to be good cousins though and to share with them always.

We headed to mass at noon, and then Elijah and Beth headed home with Hope after. They had promised Bethany's parents they'd do dinner with them this year. Sophia and Owen were having lunch with the Taylors and hanging out there for a few hours with Raelyn and Kevin before coming back to our house in the evening. Sidney was coming over around five, which meant I had plenty of time to walk Mabel, make sure the house was cleaned up, wrap up his gift, and find an outfit for tonight.

I decided the day after he and I had taken Liam to the village that I would take one of the shots of just me and him in the tunnel of lights and put it inside a clear Christmas ball. There was a store in town that customized things like this, and you could add decoration or writing as well. I had our names and the date we were there engraved on the back of the ball and chose a glittery silver ribbon for it to be hung with. I also had the photo printed and put in a red frame, and that was now sitting on my nightstand next to the photo from my birthday in Atlantic City.

I shared my gift idea with my parents, and they loved it so much, they had one created for Paityn and Liam with a picture of the two of them with Bradley. Liam gasped when they opened it together earlier this morning, and Paityn cried. I didn't know if I was expecting either of those reactions from Sidney, but hopefully it would still affect him in a special way.

When the time had finally come for him to arrive at our house, everything was ready, and Oliver and Chloe couldn't wait to meet him. They must've asked me fifteen questions about him and our dates and where I saw things going, which I didn't really mind answering, but I wanted to save some of it for when Sidney was there in person. I was curious what he would share with them and maybe how much he had thought about the future, our future.

We had seen all of our grandparents at mass, but none of them were joining us for dinner. It was starting to feel like they were getting too old to be out and about a lot. I could see myself being like that when I was in my eighties too, if not way before then. There was nothing wrong with a quiet night relaxing on a reclining chair watching a favorite film or reading a good book. And if that was what worked for them, who was I to judge?

Sophia and Owen returned from their time with the Taylor family, and Sidney had just come in, so it was now time to sit down for Christmas dinner. The table was set for ten. My dad was at one head, and my mom was at the other. Owen, Sophia, myself, and Sidney sat on one side of the table, and across from us were Paityn, Liam, Oliver, and Chloe. The night before, we had to use both the kitchen table and the dining room table with its extended leaf. We've had to do that in years past for holidays as well, but there was something nice and cozy about this meal.

"How was your Christmas Eve?" Sophia asked Sidney once we were settled and eating our appetizer salads.

"It was nice. Thank you for asking! I love getting to see my parents," he replied kindly.

"How do they feel about you moving to Doylestown and working at the hospital?" Chloe asked.

"They think it was the right move for me. Of course, they wish they could spend more time with me, but they just want me to be happy."

"Have you had the opportunity to explore a lot of the area yet?" Oliver inquired, knowing I had taken him to some of the hot spots.

"Well, luckily, I've had a really amazing tour guide." Sidney looked over at me with a cute little smirk. "Ashton knows how to show someone a good time."

"Oh, yeah? Do tell! Where have you two gone?" Oli followed up.

"I took him to Shady Brook, the vineyard Sophia loves so much, and over to the village," I told my brother.

"I went too!" Liam chimed in. "Do you still have your wand like mine?" he asked Sidney.

"Sure do! I practice casting spells every day at my apartment!"

"I do that too in the basement, but Mom puts the wand in timeout sometimes." Liam glanced over at Paityn, who was chuckling at being called out.

"He gets a little carried away with that wand," my sister said. "He tried to turn Doug into a potato a few days ago. Doug was not pleased."

Everyone laughed and began eating the main course. My mom made sure each of us had a drink, which for most of us was red wine, excluding Liam and Chloe, of course. Liam wanted apple juice, and Chloe asked for water with lemon.

"Ashton texted me this morning to give me the good news," Sidney said to Oliver and Chloe. "Congratulations. That's so exciting! I wish you guys the best."

"Thank you!" Chloe responded.

"Yes, we appreciate that," Oliver joined in. "It's a little scary, the idea of two babies at once, but I think we're up to the challenge!"

"Maybe you can come out to San Diego with me to visit them?" I asked Sidney courageously. Proposing a trip across the country together so soon might have been risky, but the words fell out of my mouth before I could stop them.

"Are you saying you'll still like me in May?" he responded, almost blushing. "I'd love to go to Cali with you. We should definitely talk about it more."

Oliver locked eyes with me from directly across the table. He smiled approvingly, which meant the absolute world to me. I could see how proud he was of me and the journey I'd been on.

And I'm proud of myself too.

AFTER DESSERT and a round of "guess who wrote the note" with the family, where each of us wrote something funny about another person in the room that we chose from a bowl and then had to figure out who penned it, Sidney and I went up to my room, where I had been keeping his gift. I told him I had something to give him and wanted to do it in private. And he shared he also had something for me, but he needed to retrieve his coat from the foyer closet before heading upstairs. Curious, my mind started conjuring ideas of things that were small enough to fit in his pocket.

I shut the door behind us, in case I wanted to sneak in a kiss or something, and I went into my desk drawer to grab the box where I kept his ornament with our photo from the tunnel. He sat down on my bed with his coat lying next to him. I sat down to the right of him and scooted in close.

"I hope you like it," I said, handing him the present.

"I'm sure I'll love whatever is inside here. Besides, it's the thought that counts," he replied, taking off the top of the box.

"I printed a copy for myself too and already put it in a frame," I told him as he picked the ball up and stared at it in the light.

"What a creative idea!" he exclaimed. "I'll probably have it hanging in my apartment all year round. Thank you!" He leaned forward to give me a soft kiss. His lips tasted like red wine and peppermint. And I wanted more. "I have yours in my coat pocket." He reached in, pulled out a white envelope, and put it in my hand.

"What's this?" I asked him, seriously having no clue of its contents.

"You'll see in a second. Open it!" he urged.

I carefully tore the envelope and saw there were two tickets inside it. I lifted them out and read the event title: Irving Berlin's White Christmas. And it was playing at the Bucks County Playhouse, on New Year's Eve.

"I love this! When did you get these?" I asked him with a huge glow on my face.

"I was searching over the last two weeks, but I picked them up yesterday before going to see my parents. I was thinking how you have taken me to some really great places in the area, but I hadn't taken you anywhere special. And then I saw on the work schedule that neither of us were on the night shift for the thirty-first."

"Sidney, this is an awesome gift. Thank you so much! It'll be such a great time."

"You're welcome!" He leaned in to kiss me again, but

this time it was longer than the last. "I was hoping I could take you to dinner before the show. Would that be okay?"

"That would be more than okay. There are so many incredible restaurants in New Hope for us to try, and I can't think of a better way to end the year than with someone as amazing as you are." I accepted his offer and then kissed him some more. I would kiss him all night if he'd allow it.

30

SOPHIA

A couple of days after Christmas, while Owen and I were in the studio adding photos to our theme books, we heard the doorbell ring. Bowie performed her adorable combination of a howl and a bark and sprinted to the apartment front window, trying to see who was there. When her tail started wagging, I knew it was someone she recognized. Two someones actually.

My sister and my mom were standing there when I opened the door, carrying a bag from the delicious bagel barn nearby, and seemingly very upbeat for so early in the morning.

What do I owe this unexpected visit? Not that I'm complaining.

They came in, and I called for Owen to join us in the kitchen, announcing the presence of family and bagels. He was with us in under a minute and turning on the Keurig, which was great because I could *always* use more coffee.

"No Liam?" I asked Paityn. "Where's the little guy?"

"Oliver and Chloe wanted to take him out for the day since they never get any time with him alone. And it's good practice for them with expecting two little boys of their own."

"I still can't believe they are having twins," I said, processing the idea even days later.

"They'll make excellent parents though," Mom said.

"So, what brings you both here this morning?" Owen asked them, serving their coffee with cream and sugar on the side.

"I realized I hadn't been over here in a long time," Paityn replied. "After we moved back, things were so chaotic, and I never stopped in to see you guys at home. I apologize for that."

"Don't be silly! You've had a lot on your plate," I told her. "And it's not like we haven't seen you."

"Thank you for giving me grace." She poured cream into her mug and then mixed in a spoonful of sugar. "The place looks even better than I remembered."

"We try to spruce things up now and again for our clients," Owen replied.

"Has this been a good location for your business?" Paityn inquired.

"It really has," I answered for both of us. "We got lucky with being on the corner of a fairly frequented block in a nice town, and there are so many places nearby with beautiful scenery to do photo shoots."

We sliced the bagels and spread on some cream cheese we had in the refrigerator. Mine was a vegetable option, since my stomach couldn't tolerate the regular stuff anymore. Then, Paityn had a few more questions about the studio and the apartment and how we had obtained the lease. We explained that Owen made an offer for the building after it was listed that was just a tad higher than what it was priced in an attempt to solidify the deal. Our realtor at the time had told Owen that someone else was interested in the property, but he really wanted it for us, so he was willing to do whatever it took, within reason. Once I was on board, we were able to sign the lease with the agent and owner of the building the following week. When we moved in, it had been newly renovated to have the current layout.

But why the sudden interest? Is this all for research in connection to her looking for a spot for the cafe she mentioned wanting to open?

"Girlfriend, what's up?" I asked her skeptically. "I feel like I shared a lot of this information when Owen and I were first moving into this place."

"You did, of course! I just don't remember all of the details, and well, if I'm being completely honest, I might have an ulterior motive for coming here today." She looked at my mom, who had just decided to focus her attention on giving Bowie a belly rub.

That's convenient.

"Okay, and what would that be? You can just say it."

"Well, you know how I mentioned wanting to open up a small restaurant around here and perhaps making it a cafe?" She led into her reasoning.

"Yes, and I think it's a great idea! Wait... are you wanting to open it right here in Doylestown?"

"I'd like to, if possible. And I thought about how you and Owen are moving to your new house soon." She dove further. "But you might need someone to sublet from you, correct?"

"Actually, we probably will need to do that, given the timing of the house settlement and the amount of months we have left on the lease here. Are you interested in being that person?" I thought that's where this was going.

I can't believe I didn't think of it myself.

"Do you guys feel like that's something we could make happen?" Paityn asked us. "It really is a great spot, and it's spacious enough. It would also save me the trouble of having to search for something."

"It would be a win-win for all of you," My mom interjected.

"Yeah, and we wouldn't live here or anything. We'd probably see if we can use some of the apartment area for a lounge and put tables out, and the bedroom could be used for a storage area."

"Wow, you've given this a lot of thought," I said. "And I love that! How about you?" I directed my attention to Owen.

"I think it could work!" he replied swiftly. "Let's talk to our agent about drawing up the paperwork and go over all of the guidelines with him."

"Thank you so much! This will help me out more than you know."

"It's honestly a perfect solution, and it feels like it's meant to be," I concluded.

It really does seem like the stars aligned to make this happen.

ON THE LAST day of the calendar year, we brought everyone over to see the dream house that we hoped would become our forever home. The move-in day was still weeks away, but with Oliver and Chloe heading back to San Diego the following afternoon, we figured taking the family today was best. And Kendal, Raelyn, and Kevin joined us too. It was almost like a party, without the food, drinks, and music.

Our realtor was kind enough to meet us there and let us in for a large group tour, and while he was there, he assured Paityn he would have the lease paperwork in order before the end of January for her to begin setting up shop. Pun intended. He had quite the sense of humor.

Hope wanted to know immediately what room would be hers when she would come to visit and sleep over. I hadn't quite figured that out yet, but there were three bedrooms, and one was right next to ours, so we discussed setting it up with two single beds for Hope and Liam to stay. This way, they could stay individually or together, and they'd be right next to us in case of any emergencies or nightmares. Though that might change if Owen and I decided to have a baby of our own one day, but we could cross that bridge if and when we were ready. And then the other room could be a guest room with a queen size bed for any adults that needed to stay. Owen suggested also having a futon somewhere for an extra place to sleep, which I wasn't against.

"This house is gorgeous," Raelyn exclaimed. "Good job, guys!"

"Thank you, Rae, but we owe a lot of credit to our agent. Sophia and I have had this on our minds for a while. She actually first said something when we were on a canoe one day back in the summer that it would be magical to live at the lake. And here we are."

"I love how you remember everything I say," I told Owen, smiling with adoration. It was so nice to know that if he had the means to make me happy, he always would.

"I hope both of you realize Kev and I will be here a lot!" Raelyn said with a laugh. "Right, hun?" Kevin nodded, not taking his eyes off the spectacular view from our window in the living room.

"I'll be here a good amount too," Kendal added. "This place is still pretty close to work and not too far from Buckingham either."

"Yup! I've been to Peace Valley a few times right after work. It's only a ten minute drive from the hospital, and it's under twenty from home," Ashton corroborated. "I'll bring Mabel here sometimes, and we can take Bowie and her for walks together."

"Whoa! Apparently, Bowie loves the sound of that! Look at that tail going a mile a minute," Owen said. "I think our girl is going to live her best life here."

"I think all of us are going to live our best lives here," I replied.

"I'm truly so happy for you," Chloe said, wandering in from the kitchen. "This house is beautiful. I can't wait to see it when we come back to visit again after you've gotten all settled in. And I can even imagine it being decorated for Christmas."

"Yeah, and by that time, we'll have two babies in tow!" Oliver called out. He and Elijah had been going from room to room checking the foundation, or at least that's what they claimed. "We'll have to keep a double stroller stored somewhere on the grounds to take the boys for walks."

"How exciting!" Mom fawned over the idea of two babies being pushed along the path by my brother. "Your father and I were just taking a peek at the surrounding area outside. Everything appears safe, and there are plenty of places to plant flowers." I hoped my mom planned on helping me with said garden duties.

We all know I don't exactly have a green thumb.

Bethany and Paityn had taken Hope and Liam to see if there were any ducks in the lake. It always surprised me how they still enjoyed being in the water even when it was cold, but I read once that they did it to stay warm and access food. When I went outside to get them, Liam was raving about how he saw one female duck and one male duck, and he was educating Hope on the difference between the two.

"The male ducks are the ones with the pretty colors, Hope. They have to be that way to attract the girl ducks."

"I think the girl ducks should be the pretty ones because girls are pretty and boys aren't," she said with strong conviction.

"That's not always true. Some boys are pretty," Ashton commented.

"Okay, buddy. She's too young to know the specifics of your dating preferences," Bethany said jokingly.

"Mommy, I already know that Uncle Ashton dates a boy. And that's okay. You said that we can love who we want to love." Hope caught on quickly to the dialogue.

"That's right, baby girl!" Bethany praised her. "It is totally acceptable for people to date whoever they choose. And I forget how intelligent you are sometimes." Hope was definitely wise beyond her years.

"Let's pray she stays that accepting and open-minded in years ahead. She's just remarkable, never wavering in her kindness and respect." I spoke in admiration of my niece but also of Eli and Beth for being such wonderful parents and raising such a bright little girl.

"Speaking of my dating life," and suddenly the entire group was together again standing in front of the house. "I'm going out with Sidney tonight for dinner and a show. It's his Christmas gift to me. I have to get home to get ready soon." Ashton hugged everyone and walked to his car.

"So does that mean we can start calling this guy your boyfriend officially?" Elijah asked, calling out to him.

"Yes!" Ashton yelled back. "Sidney is my boyfriend. Happy?"

"Only if you are!" I bellowed. But in truth, I was utterly and completely overjoyed for my baby brother. He deserved this.

And once he was gone, the rest followed, wishing us well and making us promise to give continuous updates. It was nearing the later part of the afternoon, but the sun was still shining. We had the realtor lock up, and we hooked Bowie back on to her harness and leash. As the agent drove away in his car, Owen and I stood facing the house hand in hand at the edge of the gravel driveway, taking it all in.

Bare trees swayed in the soft wind, and the sound of water slapping against the docks could be heard in the distance. The crisp air brought a sense of calm and a sense of hope for the future.

"Can you believe all of this is ours?" I asked Owen, turning to face him, the breeze blowing through my hair and his.

"It didn't feel real until just now," he whispered, kissing me on the forehead. "But we're about to live the life we imagined, Sophia. And I wouldn't want anyone else by my side."

"I love you so much," I told him, placing my head on his shoulder.

"I love you more."

EPILOGUE
ASHTON

Maya Angelou once said, "You alone are enough. You have nothing to prove to anybody." This has encouraged me to find confidence and fulfillment within myself. A person's worth is not contingent upon comparisons or the opinions of others. And it took me years to get to a place where I truly believe this.

I hardly recognize the person I was in my senior year of high school. Back then, I carried doubt like armor, skeptical that my voice, my identity, or my hopes could ever matter.

Today, I lean back into my chair in my bedroom, sunlight spilling across the page of the journal where I've chronicled everything: the setbacks, the breakthroughs, the quiet triumphs.

I've come to understand how the act of reflection – writing through my fears, tracing patterns in my behavior, examining the choices I made – wasn't just therapeutic, it was transformational.

I learned to ask the right questions. *What shaped me then? What held me back? What small victories did I over-*

look? And I answered with honesty, grace, and compassion toward my younger self.

Over these years, I built routines rooted in mindfulness. I journaled, held vulnerable conversations, and set goals with intention rather than expectation. Everything in my life changed as I changed. Boundaries felt less like defenses and more like invitations.

I'd forgiven myself for past regrets and cultivated pride in my everyday strengths. I genuinely accepted who I was and what it took for me to get there.

I now feel peace in my body and secure in my worth. I found someone who loves me for me, while making me feel both seen and heard. In his presence, I learned that love's power lies in the freedom to be fully and unapologetically me.

REVIEW REQUEST

Dear Reader,

Reviews are like currency to any author – actually, even better! As they help to get our books noticed by even more readers, we would be so grateful if you would take a moment to review this book on Amazon, Goodreads, your blog - wherever - and feel free to share it on social media!

We're not asking for any special favors – honest reviews would be perfect. They also don't need to be long or in-depth, just a few of your thoughts would be so appreciated.

Thank you greatly from the bottom of our hearts. For your time, for your support, and for being a part of our reading community. We couldn't do it without you – nor would we want to!

~ Our Firefly Hill Press Family
Unwavering Hope

ABOUT THE AUTHOR

Nelianne Genner is a high school special education literature teacher, who loves to read and write. She spends a lot of time with her family and friends and uses her experiences and relationships as inspiration for her realistic fiction work. Nelianne has a strong passion for art, dance, film, and photography. She resides in Doylestown, Pennsylvania with her husband, Curt, her retrievers, Livy and Paisley, and her rabbit, Gatsby.

Reach out to her and say hello on social media, by email, or through Firefly Hill Press!
Email: neliannegenner@gmail.com

Printed in the United States of America

Firefly Hill Press, LLC
4387 W. Swamp Rd #565
Doylestown, PA 18902
www.fireflyhillpress.com
info@fireflyhillpress.com

Print ISBN: 978-1-945495-52-6
E-Book ISBN: 978-1-945495-45-8

www.ingramcontent.com/pod-product-compliance
Lightning Source LLC
Chambersburg PA
CBHW071252250626
47159CB00004B/1149